"Where should we start?"

"Your...hair," Ethan finally managed to say.

Maggie raised her hands to her hair. "You think you can do something with this?" she asked with a smile. "Better hairdressers than you have tried. My hair seems to be hopeless."

Oh, no. Not to him. Frayed and tortured as it was, he could think of a hundred things he'd like to do with her hair. There was something very sensual about Maggie's hair that made a man itch to plunge his fingers into it. It might not be duchess hair, but it was glorious in its own way. He wanted his hands in that cool silk, his lips on the loose curls that fell across her forehead.

Her hair most definitely had to be changed.

Dear Reader,

There's no better escape than a fun, heartwarming love story from Silhouette Romance. So this August, be sure to treat yourself to all six books in our sexy, sizzling collection guaranteed to keep you glued to your beach chair.

Dive right into our fantasy-filled A TALE OF THE SEA adventure with Melissa McClone's *In Deep Waters* (SR#1608). In the second installment in the series about lost royal siblings from a magical kingdom, Kayla Waterton searches for a sunken ship, and discovers real treasure in the form of dark, seductive, modern-day pirate Captain Ben Mendoza.

Speaking of dark and seductive, Carol Grace's *Falling for the Sheik* (SR#1607) features the mesmerizing but demanding Sheik Rahman Harun, who is nursed back to health with TLC from his beautiful American nurse, Amanda Reston. Another royal has a heart-wrenching choice to make in *The Princess Has Amnesia!* (SR#1606) by award-winning author Patricia Thayer. She survived a jet crash in the mountains, but when the amnesia-stricken princess remembers her true social standing, will she—can she—forget her handsome rescuer...?

Myrna Mackenzie's *Bought by the Billionaire* (SR#1610) is a Pygmalian story starring Ethan Bennington, who has only three weeks to transform commoner Maggie Todd into a lady. While Cole Sullivan, the hunky, all-American hero in Wendy Warren's *The Oldest Virgin in Oakdale* (SR#1609), is coerced into teaching shy Eleanor Lippert how to seduce any man—himself included.

Then laugh a hundred laughs with Carolyn Greene's *First You Kiss 100 Men...* (SR#1611), a hilarious and highly sensual read about a journalist assigned to kiss 100 men. But there's only one man she *wants* to kiss....

Happy reading—and please keep in touch!

Mary-Theresa Hussey

Mary-Theresa Hussey
Senior Editor

Please address questions and book requests to:
Silhouette Reader Service
U.S.: 3010 Walden Ave., P.O. Box 1325, Buffalo, NY 14269
Canadian: P.O. Box 609, Fort Erie, Ont. L2A 5X3

Bought by
the Billionaire

MYRNA MACKENZIE

Published by Silhouette Books

America's Publisher of Contemporary Romance

To Pat White—
a great friend, a great writer and a woman who knows
how to zero in on the important things in life.

 SILHOUETTE BOOKS

ISBN 0-373-19610-5

BOUGHT BY THE BILLIONAIRE

Visit Silhouette at www.eHarlequin.com

Printed in U.S.A.

Books by Myrna Mackenzie

Silhouette Desire

The Baby Wish #1046
The Daddy List #1090
Babies and a Blue-Eyed Man #1182
The Secret Groom #1225
The Scandalous Return of Jake Walker #1256
Prince Charming's Return #1361
Simon Says... Marry Me! #1429
At the Billionaire's Bidding #1442
Contractually His #1454
The Billionaire Is Back #1520
Blind-Date Bride #1526
A Very Special Delivery #1540
Bought by the Billionaire #1610

Silhouette Books

Montana Mavericks
Just Pretending

*The Wedding Auction

MYRNA MACKENZIE,
winner of the Holt Medallion Award honoring outstand-
ing literary talent, believes there are many unsung
heroes and heroines living among us, and she loves to
write about such people. She tries to inject her charac-
ters with humor, loyalty and honor, and after many
years of writing she is still thrilled to be able to say that
she makes her living by daydreaming. Myrna lives with
her husband and two sons in the suburbs of Chicago.
During the summer she likes to take long walks, and
during cold Chicago winters she likes to *think* about taking long walks (or dream of summers in Maine).
Readers may write to Myrna at P.O. Box 225,
LaGrange, IL 60525, or they may visit her online at
www.myrnamackenzie.com.

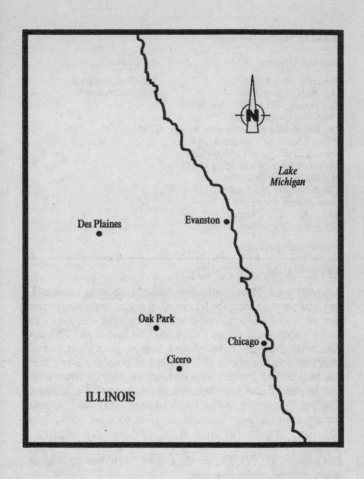

Lake
Michigan

Des Plaines
●

Evanston
●

Oak Park
●

Chicago
●

Cicero
●

ILLINOIS

N

Chapter One

"You've done a lot of wild things with women, Ethan, but trying to transform an ordinary, mortal woman into a goddess of the social scene is definitely going to be the wildest. You're sure you don't want to change your mind? Or at least choose a different woman?"

What he wanted to do, Ethan Bennington thought, was go back to his office and see to his business. But it was the fate of his business, after all, that had brought him here. He shook his head and grinned at his friend, who was gesturing to a smiling photo of a woman in the First Annual Suburban Chicago Job Auction for Charity brochure he was studying. A somewhat shapeless woman in baggy blue jeans and an oversize blue shirt pushing a broom and hauling a man-size garbage can behind her.

"Not a chance of changing my mind, Spence. And as for the woman, well, my client, Lionel Griggs, came here and chose her himself. She *has* to be a challenge if I'm to prove myself." Ethan glanced over to the row of seats where the elderly man had retired to make sure that everything proceeded successfully.

"By the way, it was you and Dylan who put the idea into Lionel's head," Ethan offered.

Dylan, his other friend, frowned. "I've never even spoken to Lionel Griggs. Not until you introduced us today."

Ethan shrugged. "If I recall correctly, you made a comment within hearing range of a reporter. Something about the fact that I had a way of elevating a woman's social standing."

Spencer exchanged looks with Dylan, and they both winced. "You do," Spencer agreed. "You pick out a woman for your bed and suddenly she's on the front page of every society rag in town. But this isn't the same thing at all, and Magdalena Todd," he said, holding out the brochure, "isn't even close to the type of woman you usually choose. I'm not sure even you can convince the world that she was born of noble blood."

Ethan smiled at his friend's offended tone, but it wasn't the lady's fault that she wasn't an exotic debutante. And she hadn't asked to be brought into this game. At the moment she didn't even have a clue that there was to be a game.

Ethan glanced around at the T-shirt-clad Saturday throng milling around the west suburban park where the auction was being held. This gathering of human beings giving up their time to the highest bidder for a worthy cause was like nothing he'd ever attended before. Still, the location was perfect. Very few people knew him this far west of the city, and anonymity was essential in this case.

"If everything doesn't work out," Spencer said,

"she could bury the Bennington name in the business world forever, Ethan."

"Or she could save the Bennington name."

"It's too risky."

Maybe so, but he didn't really have a choice.

Taking a deep breath, he squared his shoulders, then smiled tightly at Spencer and Dylan. "All right, you've warned me. Now go find your own women. I'm about to lay claim to mine."

And he walked away, searching the crowd to locate Magdalena Todd. The brochure burned hot against his skin in the sunlight, as if the words printed there had a life of their own. He didn't have to reread the darn thing to know what it said. Maggie Todd was, at twenty-five, a school custodian with no significant education other than half a semester of junior college. She didn't belong to a single club or society. Her skills included the ability to repair busted water pipes, furnaces, and to rebuild automobile engines. In other words, she was perfect for what Lionel had in mind.

And as he finally spotted her, half-hidden behind a tree, tugging at her sagging panty hose, he couldn't help smiling. Poor Magdalena. She had signed on to give her time for a good cause, and no doubt she assumed she'd be hired to repair busted pipes or to sweep floors. She might feel uncomfortable once he told her what he was planning.

Almost as uncomfortable as her panty hose were making her feel, he mused as she tugged at them again. She raised her head suddenly, as if she were afraid someone had seen.

He glanced away, long enough to give her a chance to come out from behind her tree.

"I hope you don't mind, Magdalena," he whispered as she made her way toward the risers where the auction was taking place. "But I intend to claim you before this morning is through. Lionel was right. You're perfect for this part."

As he moved closer to the risers he noticed that she was twisting her fingers into knots. Her scruffy curls were an intriguing shade of auburn that fell almost to her shoulders, but her hair had obviously been cut by either a very bad stylist or a gardener with a wickedly dull pair of shears. The white sack of a dress she wore could have once been a rumpled bedsheet or a bag for carrying potatoes in from the field. She was clearly nervous, fidgeting as she waited her turn to step onto the stage. She was…chewing gum.

At that very moment Magdalena blew a bubble that would have made any ten-year-old proud. Pink. Round. Large. It popped suddenly, and Ethan could almost read the lady's surprise as her eyes widened and she nearly crossed them, trying to see if she'd left any telltale traces on her nose.

She moved up onto the riser, and Ethan caught sight of the way the muscles in her calves tensed, the way her breasts strained a bit against the baggy cloth of her dress.

He breathed in, his nostrils flaring slightly. Like a mare sensing a stallion's presence she looked straight at him then, and as he moved closer he could tell one thing: beneath that sack of a dress, Magdalena Todd was very definitely a woman.

"Watch it, Bennington," he whispered to himself, leaning back against a tree ten feet away from the stage. He was obviously losing it. Only a few weeks ago he'd been in Ariel Tenant's bed. Ariel was, according to all known male sources, a woman to die for, and he had been willing to dutifully give his life for his fellow man. But Ariel hadn't made him feel raw and hungry. She had made him feel the way most women did these days—eager for a while and then bored. And if he was sniffing the air for the scent of an ordinary and slightly frumpy woman in a shapeless white sack, then he had clearly slipped more than even he had imagined. Besides, personal involvement wasn't allowed in this case. Deep personal involvement wasn't allowed anytime, given his past, but this situation precluded *any* type of attachment between himself and the woman, deep or otherwise.

So she was safe. Ethan smiled into the lady's eyes.

Her own eyes widened for just a second before she looked to the side, swallowing hard.

"Brown eyes," he noted to himself. Huge. And embarrassed. He could just see the barest hint of her chest rising and falling rapidly beneath the dress.

Immediately his imagination kicked in. At age thirty, he knew very well what women looked like beneath their clothes. He'd seen far more than his share of bare breasts. These would be high…and firm…a little larger than average, with coral tips…

Ethan caught himself up short. He forced himself to note the chopped-off locks of Magdalena Todd's hair, the way she was twisting uncomfortably beneath his perusal, shifting from foot to foot in those heavy black shoes she wore.

"Come on, Maggie, my dear," the auctioneer was calling. "It's your turn. Don't be shy, love."

A guffaw went up from the people on the risers. "Maggie, shy?" one man called. "You don't know our Maggie. She can make up stories or arm wrestle you to the ground when she wants to."

"Andy, I don't happen to be here to arm wrestle or spin stories today," the woman called, her voice loud enough to carry to the perimeters of the small park.

"And I'm here the same as all of you, to help the kids at Safe House so they don't end up joining a gang or living on the streets. And just so you know, I don't ever use bad language, and whoever hires me will get his or her money's worth and then some."

Her eyes were dark and earnest. She folded her arms across her chest, plumping up those soft breasts as she finished.

Ethan felt a strange urge to give a cheer for her little speech. He had read her stats in the brochure. She had worked five years at the school and only missed three days.

"Aw, Maggie, we were just kidding you," the man called out.

Ethan took another step forward, moving in front of the audience. "I'd like to start the bidding," he said.

"We haven't read off her qualifications yet," the auctioneer said. "Other than Maggie's own speech, that is."

"I've read her qualifications," Ethan said, straightening to his full height of six-three and staring the auctioneer down. He knew he could be imposing when he chose to. He chose to now.

The man frowned and swiped one hand across his brow. "It's an auction, though. We have rules."

Ethan shrugged. He noticed that Magdalena herself was nodding, as if she were afraid. Maybe she'd seen him staring at her breasts. The thought made Ethan uneasy. He didn't intend to bed the woman he hired. He wouldn't want her to worry that he was planning to hurt her in any way.

He stared up into her eyes, trying to reassure her. It must be somewhat frightening putting oneself up for auction. At least he had impeccable social credentials, even if his father had been a cad and an untrustworthy businessman. Surely he could reassure Ms. Todd that he meant her no harm once he had hired her.

But for now she was eyeing him the way a horse might eye a man with a whip. Perhaps his eagerness was distressing her.

"Easy, Ethan," he heard Dylan say in a low voice as his friends walked up behind him.

"She doesn't know what this is about. Remember she doesn't know that you're planning on waving the Bennington wand over her and making her every dream come true," Spencer agreed. "And who can blame her, man, the way you're looking at her?"

Ethan clenched his teeth. He turned slightly to look at his friends. "Just *how* am I looking at her?" he demanded, dropping his voice.

Dylan grinned.

Spencer raised one brow.

"You dogs," Ethan said. "I was not looking at her that way."

"You were. If she were Ariel Tenant, she'd be panting and taking her clothes off right now. As it is, she's a woman who's here to hire out and do a good deed for charity. I doubt that's the kind of good deed she was anticipating."

Ethan gave a curt nod. He lowered his eyelids slightly and took a deep breath.

"You're correct," he called out to the auctioneer. "There are rules. I believe quite strongly in rules." Rules were, after all, what he was going to use to transform Magdalena into the great-great-granddaughter of a duke. Rules were what his father had broken repeatedly, tumbling his marriages, the agency and years of hard work and family honor into the dirt. "Please. Tell me about the rest of Ms. Todd's qualifications."

And when the man was done, the bidding would begin.

Ethan gave Magdalena a slow smile and nodded his head deeply. He would wait and then he would bid whatever it took.

In three weeks time, both their lives would be changed, and no man was going to look at Magdalena Todd and want her to wash windows.

By then she would be his cool, dignified, soft-spoken, high-born lady, and taking her to bed would be the first thing on every man's mind.

Maggie stood in the center of the raised platform and resisted the urge to scratch the mosquito bite on her arm as Donnie began listing her qualifications. Of course, that mosquito bite might be a welcome distraction under the circumstances.

Why on earth did that beautiful, obviously well-to-do man keep staring at her that way?

She took a deep breath, causing her dress to swell up. Would this auction never end so she could get back to her comfortable jeans and gym shoes? This dress was pure torture to wear. These shoes felt like something the Spanish Inquisition would have hawked if they'd had a gift shop. And that man? What on earth was with that man? He was wearing a suit, the black jacket looped casually over one finger. He looked as if he'd just stepped out of the pages of one of those ritzy men's magazines that the teachers drooled over.

And he had wanted to bid on her before Donnie had even read off all the nice things the Safe House committee and the school board had written about her. What for? What on earth could she do for a man like that?

Maggie tried not to look at the man, but even as she

stared into the distance at an airplane circling toward Midway Airport, she could still see him in her mind. Hair as black and soft-looking as that of a puppy she'd once owned, shoulders like…well, shoulders that would probably look awfully good once he took that crisp white shirt off, and eyes—she didn't want to think about his eyes.

The plane dipped lower in the sky. Maggie forced herself to follow its path, but her mind just saw those silver eyes. They were the kind of eyes that told a woman he could unfasten a bra with his teeth and probably had. They were the kinds of eyes that had witnessed women—lots of women—in the throes of passion.

What is a man like that doing bidding on you, Maggie?

"I don't know," she muttered beneath her breath. "Maybe he needs his plumbing fixed. Even men who spend half their lives in bed have to get up and face life's more practical problems now and then."

"You don't like what I'm saying about you, Maggie?" Donnie asked. "You've got something to add?"

"No, nothing, Donnie, I'm sorry." Had anyone heard what she'd said? Obviously not, judging by the serene looks on the faces of those directly in front of her.

Maggie cleared her throat. She forced herself to stare straight into the I-can-make-you-want-me-sweetheart eyes of the man she'd been trying to avoid. After being raised with four brothers, one father and too many of her brothers' friends to even count, she had learned the art of not backing down from any male.

"See anything you like, mister?" she asked suddenly, surprising a laugh from the crowd. The man standing on the other side of her dark-haired Romeo winked and slapped his friend on the back.

"She's got your number, Ethan," he said, but the silver-eyed man only gave her a slow, sexy smile.

"I see a number of things, Ms. Todd," he said, and his voice was like a promise. "And I can assure you that you and I will do business this very day."

"What are you looking for? A cleaning woman?"

"Not exactly," the man said, his voice deep and low.

Not exactly didn't sound good. It didn't tell her anything and it set her stomach to fluttering in a completely unacceptable way.

Nevertheless, ten minutes later, she was Ethan Bennington's employee. He had offered twenty-thousand dollars for her, even before anyone else had placed a bid.

No doubt about it, Maggie thought as she stumbled off the riser, she was in big trouble here. Ethan Bennington wanted something unusual from her.

Which meant that, whatever he wanted, she probably didn't have it to give.

"I think we need to talk, Mr. Bennington," she said, as he stepped forward to meet her.

"We definitely need to talk, Ms. Todd," he agreed, holding out his hand. "We need to do many things. Let's get started."

In spite of Ethan's eagerness to get down to business, it was almost two hours later before he was actually able to call Magdalena Todd his own. The rest of the employees, it seemed, needed to be auctioned off before any transactions could be finalized. Short staffing, one teacher told him with an apologetic shrug.

It was all right, he supposed. He'd had time to speak

to Lionel, who was pleased that Ethan had succeeded in purchasing Ms. Todd, but who had not wanted to stay around to meet her.

"You've got her," he'd said. "That's all that's important. Don't want to overwhelm her by making her meet too many people right out of the box. I'll meet her later today. What you're going to tell her about her job is probably going to be startling enough," he claimed. "You think you can swing this?" He glanced from Ethan to the young woman milling around with her friends just offstage. "Could be difficult."

"That was what you wanted, wasn't it?" Ethan asked.

Lionel Griggs blinked. "Of course," he said.

"Then rest assured that I intend to succeed," Ethan told him, and the old man nodded. He left soon after. Ethan turned and studied Magdalena with her fellow volunteers.

She laughed easily, heartily, her whole body joining in the process. She fiddled with the stitching on her dress at times, and he knew she wasn't entirely at ease in this world of academia. Most interesting of all, though, was the fact that she pointedly refused to look his way.

He'd held his hand out to her after the bidding had ended. She'd looked at it as if he'd offered her a cobra to kiss. Her soft skin had barely touched his before she'd pulled back.

"I'll have to catch you later," she'd said as her gaze slid away from his. "Donnie needs me to help out with the sound system. It's a little dicey."

And she had scurried away. He'd been snubbed for a sound system. Ethan smiled to himself. If he hadn't had such an important mission in mind for Magdalena, he would have considered getting to know her better just for the entertainment value of the deal. As it was, it was time now to take up his official position as her employer.

Ethan located her auburn, choppy, shoulder-length hair in the crowd and headed her way. He came up behind her. She was wielding a hammer.

"Be with you in a minute," she said, pounding at a bit of metal. "These risers have to be dismantled and this little puppy always refuses to budge." She bent down over her project, exposing a delicious but alarmingly long length of thigh. Ethan quickly stepped behind her to keep any prying eyes from sneaking a look.

"Allow me," he said, holding out his hand for the hammer.

She paused in her work, she looked at his hand, then she focused on his white shirt and tie. A hint of a smile chased away the wary expression on her face.

"Mr. Bennington, no offense, but I am a woman who wields a hammer nine days out of ten. You no doubt wield a lot of power, but it's not the kind of power you hold in your hand. There, got it," she said, freeing the stuck joint and straightening to a stand. "What do you want with me?" she asked when she looked up into his smile. "Did you make a bet with your friends?"

"In a way. I promised someone that I'd make you a princess, or near enough to a princess," he told her truthfully.

She looked up into his eyes, and he realized how much taller than her he really was. "I don't understand."

"It's very simple," he said, sliding his hand beneath her elbow and taking the hammer from her. "I'm in advertising. I create images for products. Right now I'm trying to win a potential client's business. I want to sell the man on the idea that I can help him present his restaurants in an entirely different light from how the world presently envisions them. That's where you come in. You've got a very definite set of skills,'' he said, waving the hammer around. ''Practical skills. People know they can come to you for certain things and you'll deliver, just as they know that they can go to Lionel's restaurants and get a good, wholesome, no-nonsense meal.''

''He doesn't want them to think that?''

He tilted his head. ''He wants them to see something more upscale. And he knows that if he tries to change his image and fails, he'll have lost the opportunity. He can only do it once, so it has to be done right. I have to prove to him that I can nail it on the first try.''

The lady frowned. ''So how do I fit in this picture?''

Ethan didn't blame her for seeming perturbed. ''We get one try,'' he said, his voice low. ''We take your image, and we change it. We create an illusion. When people look at you, I want them to see Magdalena Todd, a woman who feels perfectly at home wearing diamonds on a day-to-day basis. I want them to see a woman who can host a dinner party for five hundred of the city's elite and who can make each person at that party feel special. I want them to see a woman who was born on a pedestal and feels at home there, a woman who knows she was made to be adored, a woman who is equally comfortable flirting with kings or aiding the poor she's sworn to look out for.''

Those warm brown eyes took on an impudent tilt. A smile lifted the lady's lips. ''That's certainly an interesting plan. But…I hope you're not risking much on this venture. Are you?''

''I'm risking…a little,'' he acknowledged.

"How much exactly would 'a little' be?" She stood her ground and tilted her head back.

"My business," he said calmly. At her slight gasp, he reached out and touched her lips to get them to close. They did, sliding away from his fingers. "But don't worry, Ms. Todd, the business was lost several years ago. This venture is meant to bring it back. *You're* meant to help me bring it back."

"And how exactly do I do that?"

"You let me teach you what you need to know. You let me work a little magic with what you already have."

He reached out and touched a strand of her hair. It was softer than its jagged, tortured status would have led him to believe. It lay bright against his palm, tethering her to him.

She swallowed and shook her head vehemently. "I'm not the right person for this job," she finally managed to say.

"Oh, but you are," he whispered.

But still her eyes were dark and haunted. "You're frightened to work for me. Why?" he asked. "I promise you, I won't do you any harm, Ms. Todd."

"I'm not Ms. Todd," she whispered. "That's the point. I'm not even Magdalena. No one calls me that. Just Maggie. And Maggie Todd doesn't flirt with kings or with anyone else."

Her voice shook slightly. She looked just the tiniest bit frightened and unsure, and Ethan nearly swore. He was reminded that Maggie Todd was a person, not just a business proposition. He cursed himself. She was probably nervous because…well, what woman wouldn't be? What he was telling her would sound crazy to any sane human being. How could he convince her?

He looked down at her smile gracing the brochure he'd salvaged from the auction. "What's your greatest dream in life?" he asked suddenly.

"My dreams?" she asked, clearly bewildered.

He nodded slightly. "Mine is to rebuild my family's business, to prove that I'm a man who can be counted on completely. You don't have a dream? Not one?"

"I...I guess I don't believe much in dreams. I suppose what I want most is to be able to send my younger brother to college. I had to drop out in order to help the family. I want him to do things differently. If I can work hard enough, maybe I can save enough to get him started...."

Her voice fell away. Ethan realized that he was smiling.

"I know it's not much of a dream," she said.

"It's a perfect dream," he said. "Come work for me for the next three weeks, Maggie," he urged. "I'll make sure your brother can afford whatever college he wants to apply to."

She was looking up at him, sudden hope on her face.

"You would help Will?"

Ethan cursed himself. This was such a small thing she was asking for. "I'll definitely help Will."

She hesitated for several seconds. Finally she looked up at him and took a deep breath. "What if I fail?" she asked.

"You won't," he promised. "I'll make sure you don't."

She laughed then. "You're very sure of yourself, aren't you, Mr. Bennington? Is there anything on earth that you've failed to get once you set your mind to it?"

So many things. So many memories he refused to allow himself.

"I'm very determined," he said.

"And I'm very, well, often I'm completely unlady-like. But I'll let you try to work some magic with me. I'll do my best, but promise me that if this doesn't work, you won't hold it against the auction and demand your money back."

"I'm going to get my money's worth, Maggie," he promised her. "Oh yes, I am. As sure as you're a woman and I'm a man."

She swallowed hard. "I've never been much of a woman, Mr. Bennington," she said, licking her lips.

"You seem to have all the right parts to me, Maggie," he drawled.

"Parts aren't everything," she told him.

He couldn't help smiling.

"Come on, Maggie. Let's go." He took her hand, feeling the smooth slide of her skin against his fingers, but when he moved forward, she didn't move with him.

He looked down, a question in his eyes.

"How will you…you know? How are you going to know if you—if we've succeeded?"

"Lionel is having a ball for a thousand guests. You'll be the guest of honor, the great-great-granddaughter of the last Duke of Tarrington. All we have to do is fool a thousand people and we're home free. You just have to procure an invitation to the small private party the mayor throws every August."

Maggie stopped dead in her tracks.

"Mr. Bennington? Is there any insanity in your family?"

He looked down and found that she was studying him with genuine concern. She touched his arm as if he were a helpless puppy or a man with less than half a brain.

"I'm as sane as any man," he promised.

But standing there, staring down into warm brown

eyes, Ethan felt a sudden urge to lean closer to Maggie Todd just to breathe in the clean scent of her. An urge much stronger than any urge he'd ever felt in his life. Sudden heat flowed through him, though there was a cooling breeze rushing over his skin. Maybe Maggie was right. This project, the past few years since his grandfather's death—or something else, was driving him mad.

He hoped the something else wasn't the woman by his side.

Chapter Two

Hours later, after Donnie had made several calls and declared Ethan "safe," and after she'd gone home to pack her things, Maggie sat, clutching the leather seat of Ethan Bennington's Rolls-Royce. She was trying her best to pretend that her heart wasn't misbehaving. But when she glanced at Ethan out of the corner of her eye, her heart began its frantic thumping again. The man in the driver's seat was still just as stunningly handsome as he had been when she'd noticed him at the auction. And she was still just as stunningly awkward.

Which is why he wants you, she reminded herself. Because he wants to prove that he can train a lopsided egg like you to hatch out into an elegant swan.

The hysterical need to laugh rose up within her.

"Could you stop the car, please?" she asked, straining forward as Ethan turned down a long, tree-draped driveway. What looked to be a palace was waiting at the end of the driveway.

She glanced at Ethan, who raised one questioning

brow. "There's a reason, I presume, why you want me to stop the car?"

"I've changed my mind."

"What about Will?"

"We'll manage."

"And what do you intend to do when I stop the car?"

"Hitch a ride back."

"Not a good idea." He smiled indulgently, showing attractive white teeth and an achingly sexy set of dimples.

"I've done it before," she said.

His smile disappeared. "It's not safe," he said.

"I'm a grown woman."

"Still not safe." No wonder the man got whatever he wanted. Besides being rich, he was incredibly stubborn.

"You could take me home." She hoped she sounded persuasive and not childish.

"And why would I want to do that, Maggie?" Her name sounded like a soft caress on his lips. No man had ever said her name like that. He could probably make a fortune, if he didn't already have one, just by getting women to pay him to whisper their names.

She struggled to clear her thoughts. "You...you wouldn't want an unwilling employee, would you?"

At that, he swore beneath his breath and pulled the car over to the side of the driveway. "Maggie, what's wrong?" And his voice was so low and worried that she thought she just might mess up and open up to tell him what was really wrong, what she'd remembered when she'd seen this car and that house. She wasn't like other women. Growing up a total tomboy, she'd had that brought home to her time and time again. Hadn't the man she'd once worshiped left her for a woman who knew what to do with the parts God had given her? Hadn't her fiancé changed his mind about marrying her? She hadn't been able to fool even one man into thinking she was the perfect woman. How was she supposed to fool a thousand people? Couldn't Ethan see that this situation was a recipe for humiliation and disaster?

She looked at him helplessly. She bit her lip.

"Maggie?"

"I've…well, I've had time to think now, and I just can't do this. It's crazy to think that I could ever fool people into thinking that I'm somehow related to nobility."

"We, Maggie. We. I'm not going to desert you, you know." And he reached over and took her hand in his own. His hand was large and warm as his thumb stroked her palm. "I promise I'll be your safety net," he whispered, and she could just imagine him using that tone, talking a virgin right out of her tight-necked nightie without any problem at all.

She wanted to believe him, but she'd wanted to believe other things before—and been denied. "Your house," she said, looking down the driveway at the stark and imposing beauty of the elegant building. "It's so…" Words failed her.

"It's just a house," he said.

A small chuckle escaped her. It echoed through her body and made the sensitive skin of her palm slide against his. She was suddenly very conscious of the fact that she was having difficulty breathing normally. Still, she turned to look at him and rolled her eyes. "*Just* a house?"

"Okay, it's a very big house, but it can't hurt you."

"I'm not afraid," she said, raising her chin. And he smiled at her, lifting one brow slightly.

"All right, I'm afraid, but…wouldn't you be?"

"You're probably right," he conceded. "So…we'll start small. Just a few rooms at a time. One lesson at a time. When you feel overwhelmed, you'll tell me. I'll help you."

He could help her all he wanted. It wouldn't change who she was. She pulled her hand from his, took a long deep breath and started to shake her head.

"I *need* you, Maggie. Please."

Oh no, he'd gone and done it now. He'd discovered her soft spot. She couldn't turn away from someone who needed her.

"You don't need me. You could hire anyone."

"Anyone wouldn't be you. You were chosen for me. And you're unique."

Oh yes, and she didn't want to even think about what that last comment meant. But she did.

"You mean I obviously don't fit in here."

He tucked one hand beneath her chin and gently turned her to face him. "It's not a crime. We all 'fit' in different places, depending on our circumstances."

"Yes, but now you want to change me."

He shook his head. "I want to train you for a role. Consider this an acting job. Didn't you ever have a yen to take to the stage? Not even a tiny one?"

Darn the man, he definitely had her number now. She'd never stepped out on a stage in her life, not as an actor, but she had managed the stage lights for the school plays for the past five years, and she loved watching the teachers and their charges put on shows. She'd wished at times that she could join in their fun.

"It's only for a few weeks," he coaxed, gazing down at her, and she couldn't look away. Those silver eyes were so knowing, so mesmerizing. How could she lie and say she wasn't tempted?

"I—"

"Three weeks, and you'll have Will's tuition paid."

"Why does this mean so much to you?" she asked suddenly.

And his eyes turned dark. He released her. "My grandfather started an ad agency, a creative business, something I loved. My father, though, began to change things after my grandfather died. He was a creative man, too, but as time passed, he became obsessed with money and power, and he was willing to cut corners to get more of both. Eventually we argued, and he cut me out of the business. When he died six months ago, the Bennington Agency was in tatters, and clients are wary of returning. Lionel Griggs is a very big account. He's an influential man. Landing him as a client would induce others to follow."

Maggie frowned. "Your business is failing, but—" She gestured toward the house, confusion in her eyes.

Ethan nodded. "I have money left to me by my mother, but the agency is my history, my grandfather's soul, his love and legacy. Besides, money doesn't mean much without pride or a sense of accomplishment."

She understood that completely. Helping a rich man make more money wasn't any incentive for her, but helping a man regain the pride he'd lost? She groaned and slid down deeper into the plush seat. "What if I screw things up?"

He chuckled. "Then I'm back where I began. I'll still have my house and my money."

"But you won't have your pride," she whispered. "You won't have the business your grandfather built and that you clearly are passionate about. I can understand wanting that connection with him." She'd often wished she could make connections to her missing past.

"This desire to rebuild your agency—you want to make your grandfather proud of you, don't you?"

Ethan raised one brow. "It's a bit late for that."

"You think so? You think he doesn't watch over you and see what you do?"

His grin was sudden and devastatingly wicked. "*That* could be a bit embarrassing at times."

She was awfully glad she didn't blush too easily.

"I'm sure your grandfather would be a gentleman and close his eyes at times, but...I like to think that when someone we love dies, they watch over us. If you accomplish your goal, your grandfather will know. I'm sure he'll be proud."

Ethan tilted his head. He leaned closer. "You're going to help me then, aren't you, Maggie?" His voice had dropped low. It made her want to lean closer and feel his warm breath on her ear. She knew better than to give in to anything she wanted where a man was concerned. She'd learned the danger of letting herself feel. But right now she felt like a different person, not like herself at all.

The thought brought her bolt upright. Trying to be someone other than the person she was born to be had only ever brought her heartbreak and embarrassment.

But Ethan was looking at her with those beautiful silver eyes. Acting, he had said. She would get to try acting.

"It wouldn't be for long?" she asked.

"Lionel has scheduled the ball and your debut for three weeks from today. There's hardly enough time to get ready, and not enough time for you to have time to worry."

He obviously didn't know her. As she leaned forward and whispered "Yes," she was already worrying.

A lot. The next three weeks stretched before her like a nightmare obstacle path.

At the other end of the path, Ethan stood, and he was going to witness every embarrassing move she made.

The man had a butler. He had servants. Maggie's mouth fell open as she preceded Ethan into his house and gazed up at the decorative plaster carvings on the ceiling high above.

She felt like Alice drinking and eating things marked Eat Me and Drink Me as she moved farther into the room. The day had already been so strange. Now here she was, in an ultraexclusive lakeside neighborhood in the northern suburbs. Wonderland, or maybe Oz. Whichever one it was, she was certainly out of her element. Her cloddy shoes announced that fact by banging against the marble floor.

"Thank you, Walter," Ethan said, turning Maggie's bag over to the man who had let them in. "Allow me to introduce Maggie Todd. She'll be our guest for the next few weeks. Walter pretty much runs the show around here and serves as my conscience when I need one," he explained.

"Welcome, Ms. Todd," Walter said stiffly, as she smiled at him and shoved out her hand. He glanced down at her outstretched fingers. Uh-oh. Was there some rule about not shaking the hands of servants? Oh, drat. Probably there was, and now she'd gone and broken it. She was already starting out wrong. But just as she was about to snatch her hand away, Walter gave her a curt nod, a rusty half smile and took her hand for half a second. "I'll just go fix a place for you," he said, carrying her bag with him.

"The turquoise room, Walter," Ethan said, and Walter halted. He raised his brows high.

"Maggie thinks our house is rather…big," Ethan explained. "And she's absolutely right. So we'll keep things to the first floor for now. Besides, the turquoise room is smaller, a bit more comfortable. I promised you I wouldn't overwhelm you right away," he said, turning those mesmerizing eyes on her.

She felt a moment of gratitude at his understanding. If she was on the first floor and all the other bedrooms were upstairs, perhaps she wouldn't be so nervous, knowing that this beautiful man, who obviously knew his way around a woman, was right down the hall. She also wouldn't have to know if he was sleeping with someone.

What an awful thing to think. Thank goodness Ethan couldn't read her mind. No matter what happened, he mustn't think she was attracted to him. Heavens, she didn't *want* to be attracted to him, not given the way her past two relationships had ended. And not given who he was…and who she was.

"Thank you—for being understanding," she managed to say. "I'm kind of out of my depth here. But then you knew that. It's why you picked me, wasn't it?"

She fought the urge to twist her fingers together.

"You'll be comfortable, Maggie," he said softly. "In time. That's the idea."

She nodded as he began to lead her on a short tour of the first floor, but a few minutes later the sound of scuffling on the stairs made her twirl around. Walter and another man could be seen above, wrestling a bed down the huge staircase.

"Ethan?" she asked.

He chuckled. "The turquoise room is a small parlor,

Maggie. You wouldn't want to sleep on the couch. Believe me, I've tried it once or twice. Definitely not comfortable.''

He had decided to make the room comfortable for her. So she wouldn't have to face more than one floor at a time in this monster house.

She turned a smile of thanks on him. He studied her for long seconds as if she were a painting. No question what he was seeing. Ragged hair that had never obeyed a comb. Nondescript brown eyes, an uneven complexion, very ordinary features, except that her lips were too wide. Her figure looked nothing like a model's, and she could easily stand to lose ten pounds. She could probably pass for one of the servants in this house. For a moment Maggie was reminded of a Regency romance she'd read, one where the master of the house had a thing for the serving girls.

Heat suffused her body. Her smile faded.

"We'd better get you fed," he said, his voice suddenly clipped, his lashes dipping low to hide the silver of his eyes. "We'll want to be ready. Lionel told me that he'd like to meet you once you got settled in. He'll be here soon."

All thoughts of slipping around with the master of the house fled. "Lionel? He's the man who wants you to try to change me into a duchess, isn't he?"

He raised his head, and she wondered what he'd heard in her voice. His gaze was filled with concern.

"It's only an act," he said. "Remember, you'll still be Maggie Todd when this is done. With all of her assets."

His words reminded her of her fiancé, Barry telling her that they could still be friends after he'd just decided he couldn't marry her.

"Of course I will," she said, pushing away that

nasty, irrelevant thought and pasting on the bright smile she'd learned how to perfect. She used the buddy smile, the brash and slightly loud and reassuring buddy voice that she used with her brothers and all of their friends. The one that said she was just as gruff and impervious as they were.

Only, Ethan wasn't smiling back in relief the way he was supposed to. If anything, the frown that marred his beautiful forehead deepened. Maybe he was regretting this deal already. And if the deal fell through, Will might not go to college. The Safe House wouldn't get its money. She didn't want Ethan thinking she couldn't manage this task. She could manage anything, couldn't she? When a job needed doing, she did it, no matter how tough. The fact that this job was the scariest one she'd ever been on, and her employer was making both her stomach and her heart lurch couldn't matter one bit.

Soon enough she would be back at her own tasks at the school. She was lucky that they had let her go for a few weeks during the summer. And once she was back, no doubt she would look back on this time as an adventure. Something to tell the guys at work, who'd no doubt tease her about her days of playing a noblewoman.

"We'd better get ready," she said firmly. "What do we need to do before Lionel comes?"

Ethan blinked and shook his head. "Well, the first thing we do is get you fed. I have the feeling you haven't eaten anything since breakfast."

Okay, she could do that. Eating was one of her greatest skills. "All right," she agreed, tapping her finger as if she were counting off tasks. "And then what do we do?"

Grinning, Ethan crossed his arms, the muscles evident beneath his white shirt. "We wait," he said in a low voice.

"You don't want me to try to make myself look more duchesslike? Do something with my hair maybe?"

Ethan studied her hair. He shifted uncomfortably. "No, not yet. Lionel isn't expecting you to be—"

He held out his hand, palm up. "Lionel chose you at the auction, and it's not necessary to impress him."

Suddenly she got it, and her breath left her in a whoosh. She forced herself to take in air. "You want him to remember me up close as I am now. The 'before' picture so that he'll see the contrast when we get to the 'after.'"

Ethan opened his mouth. His eyes were dark. "It's not going to be that way, Maggie. You're a person, not a thing. You have value in your own right, you clearly have friends who know you well and love you for who and what you are, so don't think I'm here to hold you up to ridicule or laughter. This is, as I said, just an act."

"We're going to create a new image," she said, using his own words. "A believable illusion." And for some reason she believed him. For some reason that she couldn't fathom, he had a fear of hurting her feelings. There wasn't a reason in the world why. He didn't know her, they weren't even going to be together that long, but...

"I think I might enjoy acting," she said, sitting down on the nearest chair and preparing to wait. Waiting was something she had never been good at. She smiled up at Ethan with great determination, willing him to forget her moment of fear and weakness just moments ago.

"I hope you'll get some fun out of this," he said,

smiling back at her. "Let's think of it as a conspiracy. You and me against the world."

There was something warm and enveloping about that thought.

"Sounds good."

"All right. Let's go eat."

She put her hand in his and followed him to the kitchen.

Forty minutes later they were back in the huge blue drawing room waiting for Lionel. Maggie sat on her chair, drumming her fingers on the arm. She reached in her pocket and pulled out two pieces of bubble gum. She offered one to Ethan, who grinned broadly, thanked her and shook his head.

She shrugged, unwrapped the other piece of gum and popped it into her mouth. She shifted on her chair, then shifted again.

"Maggie," Ethan began, but her nervousness was too great to listen.

"Why don't I do something?" she said all of a sudden, jumping up. "I could…straighten my room."

He grinned. "Patience isn't a virtue?" he asked.

"*Patience* isn't even a word in my dictionary, I'm afraid."

"All right." He rose to his feet, his beautiful length towering over her. "We'll straighten your room."

She took in too deep a breath and ended up coughing. Ethan in her room might not be a good idea. He wouldn't be thinking the wrong kind of thoughts, but she just might. And if she was thinking embarrassing thoughts, she might do something stupid. She had been known to blurt out really dumb things when she was nervous.

"That's okay. I'll wait," she said, sitting down again.

But just then the doorbell sounded through the house. She gasped and nearly swallowed her gum, then rushed to find a tissue to throw it into the closest wastebasket. Her breathing was more than a touch erratic.

Ethan flashed her a reassuring smile. "Just be yourself, Maggie," he told her. "Lionel already knows a fair amount about you from the auction brochure." He touched her arm reassuringly, making her skin burn, then turned toward the door and his guest.

He crossed the floor to meet the man Walter was showing in.

"Lionel, come in. Maggie's waiting for you."

The old man strode in, an imperious look on his face, as if this house belonged to him. His gaze shifted to Maggie, who had finally landed in a chair. He looked at her as if she were a statue and he was searching for cracks.

Under his scrutiny, knowing she was on display, Maggie couldn't just sit there. She dived in, almost leaping to her feet as she bounded toward the man and shoved out her hand. "Hello, Mr. Griggs. I'm Maggie Todd."

Lionel nodded slowly, appraisingly. He didn't smile. "Maggie Todd? A custodian, aren't you?"

She nodded.

"You have...family?"

"Four brothers, a father." She wondered what these things mattered if he was here to make sure she was suitably unduchess-like enough to ensure that Ethan was starting off with really rough clay.

"That's good," he said gruffly. "Ethan, here, might not agree with me. I hear his family was no prize. His father was worthless."

Maggie almost gasped. Her gaze slid to Ethan, who remained motionless, expressionless.

"Your family, are they going to make a fuss about this setup?" Lionel demanded of her.

But Ethan stepped forward then. He smiled down at Maggie. "Family's important," he said softly. "Yours knows where you are, don't they?" he suddenly asked her, a touch of concern in his voice. "Lionel is right. I'd hate to have them worrying about you," he said, although Lionel's attitude had sounded irritated, not worried.

She raised her chin. "I'm a grown woman," she said. Just in case no one had noticed, which they sometimes didn't.

Lionel laughed, a sharp, hornlike sound. "She's got a bit of stubborn defiance in her. That's good. She'll need it to stand up to all those old biddies who are going to jump on her every flaw. Are you up to what this job entails, missy?"

"Don't badger her, Lionel. This is her first day."

"If she's going to pass the test, she has to be up to a lot. If you're going to give me what I want, you're going to have to push her."

Still, Ethan didn't move. He gazed down at her, steel in his stance. He looked as if he was going to protest again.

She shook her head. "This is part of the deal," she said. "I spend every day with a lot of men doing a lot of hard jobs, Ethan. I know how to hold my own. Even if Mr. Griggs is inclined to swear and spit."

Lionel choked and Maggie pounded him on the back. Ethan grinned and winked at her.

"Now, Mr. Griggs, what is it you want to know? Whether I can be a frog one week and a dainty flower three weeks later?"

"You're not the one on trial here," he complained, frowning at Ethan, but she knew that he was wrong.

She waited.

"I know Ethan's reputation." Lionel explained. "He's known as a man who makes women happy, not one who badgers or hurts them. I don't see how he can take a woman and tell her he wants to turn her inside out and change everything about her without hurting her. He's smart enough to have already thought of that. He's going to be watching you closely. Are you going to be able to go through with this or are you going to go running home wailing?"

She studied him, the way his gaze was too intent, like a hawk waiting for a meal. This setup, weird as it was, was definitely important to him. He blinked, and because she'd been watching him so closely, she caught his small hesitant slip, the only real trace of nervousness she'd seen in him.

"You want Ethan to win, don't you?" she asked suddenly.

Lionel Grigg's eyes flickered ever so slightly.

"You do. You want him to win."

The old man coughed, frowned, his brows nearly meeting. "If Ethan wins, I win. But it's not going to be easy for him or for you. Not at all."

"I take it there's a lot of money at stake?"

He cackled. "An obscene amount. Can you do it?"

She'd always enjoyed challenges, and her automatic response should have been yes. But it wasn't an easy question to answer. To have a man look at her every day and find her wanting would be difficult, especially given the fact that she'd already lived through that very situation in an all too personal way before. To have a man demand that she change herself completely because what she was just wouldn't do—an ordinary woman would not be able to do that.

Maggie took a deep breath. "I don't expect this to

be easy, but I'm not like other women, Mr. Griggs. I've been raised with four bar-fight-and-brawl kind of men. They love me to death, but they're not exactly shy about saying what they mean. I've had my feelings trampled and gored by well-meaning brothers who were 'just telling me for my own good' more times than I can remember. I can take anything that Ethan throws my way without tears or frowns. He won't even know if he hurts my feelings. I'm a master at hiding my feelings.'' And she wasn't lying. When Barry had told her she wasn't the woman he wanted, she had put on a master performance of not caring.

She sneaked a glance at Ethan and discovered a look of concern in his expression. She flashed him her best smile.

He frowned harder.

''We're going to win,'' she told him, and he finally smiled back at her.

''Absolutely,'' he told her in a firm voice that brooked no argument.

Lionel gave a grunt of assent. ''That's all I wanted to know, that you'd convinced her,'' he said, and he nodded to her and indicated to Ethan that he wanted to leave.

''I'll see you out,'' Ethan said. ''Will you be all right?'' he asked Maggie, and the way he paused and looked at her as if her every word and thought and concern mattered sent a flash of heat and distress spinning through her.

''I'm always all right,'' she lied. ''I'll just go to my room.'' And try not to think about the fact that she would be spending her next three weeks with a gorgeous, dark-haired stranger who was born to a class she'd never even encountered and would never encounter again when this charade was over. He would teach her how to flirt with kings. And she would do her best not to wonder what those sexy, silver eyes of Ethan's would look like at kissing range.

Chapter Three

Ethan knocked at Maggie's door and entered when she called to him. The turquoise parlor had always been cozy, but now with the oversize bed looming large between him and the woman standing at the window, the room seemed…intimate. The bed practically begged to be used for pleasure. And that was a thought he had no business pursuing.

Maggie's gaze dipped to the mattress, then darted away like a hummingbird in frantic flight.

"We can move you upstairs to something larger if you wish," he said. "There are twenty bedrooms. Enough for you to sleep in a different one almost every night you're here with me."

Her eyelids flickered. Ethan tried not to think about Maggie sleeping anywhere within his range.

Suddenly she reached into her pocket and pulled out a stick of gum. She unwrapped it and began to chew.

She's nervous, he thought. Damn it, I'm just making her nervous. This whole situation must be terrible for her.

"Maggie," he said, concern in his voice. He rounded the bed and moved nearer to her.

That was obviously the wrong thing to do. Those huge picture-window eyes of hers registered panic. She chewed her gum faster. And then she smiled, a smile so forced that Ethan would have been amused if he hadn't known that he was the reason she felt she had to pretend.

"Oh, no. The room is fine. I'm fine."

How could he believe that? "Maggie?"

"No, really, this is all very…nice. Now, about this noblewoman stuff. Just how difficult do you think this will be?"

Ethan blinked at the sudden change in subject, but he welcomed it. "Well," he said, taking a deep breath. "I'd be lying if I told you it would be easy. The rich can sometimes be difficult. And then, of course, there's the truth serum factor. Have you ever had to romance a thousand people while lying a thousand lies?"

She shook her head vigorously. "Not this year."

He smiled. So did she. "But I'll give it all I've got."

"That's more than anyone has a right to ask, Maggie."

She frowned. "No, you paid a lot of money for me to be here. What exactly did you mean by the rich being difficult?"

He shrugged. "Judgmental?"

"That's what I thought. I guess I'll have to watch myself. I've always been a bit hardheaded and inclined to kick. My father used to say that I was a handful. I'm guessing that wouldn't be a good character trait to exhibit now."

Ethan grinned. "Might be interesting."

But Maggie didn't smile. "I meant what I said,

Ethan. I know what's at stake here, and I'll do my best to help you win your heart's desire.''

Ethan's breath caught when she said the word *desire,* and he saw her blink. She looked uncertain, as if she'd known what his reaction had been and she regretted her choice of words.

"Well, then.'' She blew out a breath that ruffled her bangs. "That Lionel is pretty intense, but he doesn't seem so completely terrible, does he?'' she said, rushing on.

Ethan shook his head, wondering why it seemed that Maggie was trying to reassure him rather than the other way around.

"He's just a man with a mission,'' he agreed.

"And he's worried that we won't be able to make this work.'' She chewed her gum more furiously. "I think we should probably get straight to work if we're going to have time to make me over. What do you think we should change first?''

Her earnest brown eyes had green highlights, he realized, then wished he hadn't noticed. But he had.

She chewed her gum. Ethan cast around for some way to relieve her tension, to set things back on an even keel. Where should they start on this task they'd set out on together?

Suddenly he picked up a garbage can and handed it to her. "Maybe we should get rid of the gum,'' he said with a wink.

She did, then clasped her hands behind her back and looked up at him. "Okay,'' she said. "But I have to tell you that I chew gum because I tend to talk too much when I'm not sure what I'm doing. No doubt about it, I'm going to run into plenty of situations at the ball where I don't know what I'm doing. So…how do I keep my mouth in line if I'm not chewing gum?''

He groaned. He tried not to let his thoughts run wild, but he lost the battle. Leaning forward, he touched his lips to hers. Lightly. Her lips parted beneath his and he fought to keep from deepening the kiss. Somehow he managed to pull away.

"You keep your lips together," he said, his voice a shade too thick. "At least the first time a man kisses you."

She gazed up at him, her expression slightly dazed. She swallowed. "Do you—do you really think there are going to be men kissing me?"

As if she trusted him not to do it again. And she damn well ought to be able to trust him.

"At the ball," he managed to say. "They'll try."

Hours later Ethan was still thinking of what an idiot he'd been. Touching her when she was here under his protection. He'd seen confusion in her eyes. And he hadn't even apologized. Because he'd been wanting to taste her since the moment he'd seen her on that stage. So he'd kissed her. And now he wanted to do it again.

That would be a bad idea. There was something about Maggie that made him reckless, and that couldn't be allowed. He'd known for years that he didn't want to play with the complicated fire of commitment. Not that he was at risk. He hadn't felt anything deeply in ages, but he'd seen his father ruin women's lives thoughtlessly. His first wife. His second. His third.

Still, his father's messes weren't the biggest reason Ethan always left before emotions had a chance to take root. After watching his father's tactics, he'd thought he would be different, and yet he hadn't been. His engagement to Vanessa was to have been a mere matter of business. But she'd fallen in love. And instead of doing the right thing and leaving while her emotions were new and weak, he'd stayed and tried to force himself to feel. Eventually she'd seen the lie. They'd parted. But not before her youth, her ideals and her heart had been damaged. Needlessly.

It had been a serious lesson to him. If a relationship threatened to spiral out of control, it was time to move on.

But when he closed his eyes, control slipped away and all he could think of was how Maggie's lips had felt beneath his.

Groaning, Ethan rolled out of bed and grabbed up a black silk robe. In the kitchen lay the solace of a midnight snack to chase away the demons of forbidden desire.

Rushing down the stairs, he rounded the banister— and smacked into something that hadn't been there in the past.

It was soft, it had satiny skin that pleased his fingertips. Maggie, he thought as the woman scent of her filled his nostrils, as his body connected with hers. She gasped with a delightful, breathy sound.

"Maggie," he whispered, reaching out and clutching her to him to check for breaks in her arms, in her legs.

"Ethan?" She moaned slightly as he touched the place where he must have slammed into her.

"Aw, damn, I've hurt you," he whispered, running his hands up to examine the silk of her throat, her chin, the bridge of her nose as he searched for the damage he'd done.

She dragged in a deep, shuddery breath, then stepped away. "No, no, I'm…I'm fine. I was just…I couldn't sleep. The bed—the room is so much bigger than what I'm used to."

He tried to chase away the vision of her lying there in a bed big enough for two people intent on enjoying each other.

"I was looking for the kitchen," she said, "but I guess I got lost."

He smiled in the dark. She sounded so forlorn.

"I'll take you there," he said. "We'll see what we can find." Trying not to touch her, he led her to the kitchen and snapped on the light.

She was wearing a chenille bathrobe of pale blue with a hole just beneath the collar. It should have looked ratty. Somehow it didn't, clinging to her curves and demonstrating that yes, she did indeed have a body that could make a man beg for ice water. Not a noblewoman's body, but right now Ethan wasn't exactly thinking about nobility.

He dragged his gaze up to her face. She was looking at him expectantly, waiting for him to say something.

Reality intruded like a cold rain. He was here to be her mentor. She was to be his student. No more than that.

"I'll get you something to eat," he said gently. "Then since we're both up, we might as well get started on what we brought you here to do. Planning our strategy."

She looked up at him with dark eyes and nodded slowly. "That would be best, I think. Where should we start?"

By finding you something to wear that doesn't make me want to look beneath your clothing, he wanted to say. Instead, he forced himself to think, to move toward safer waters.

"Your...hair," he finally managed to say.

She raised her hands to her hair with a look of wonder. "You think you can do something with this?" she asked with a smile. "Better hairdressers than you have tried. My hair seems to be hopeless."

Oh no. Not to him. Frayed and tortured as it was,

he could think of a hundred things he'd like to do with her hair. Starting with touching it, having it fall over him. Her hair had the look, he finally realized, of a woman's hair when a man had gotten his fill of her, after he'd made love to her and mussed it badly. After he'd tangled his fingers in the soft stuff for hours as he lost himself in her body. There was something very sensual about Maggie's hair that made a man itch to plunge his fingers into it. It might not be duchess hair, but it was glorious in its own way, and it very much belonged in a bedroom on a naked Maggie. He saw her that way, he wanted his hands in that cool silk, his lips on the loose curls that fell across her forehead as his flesh met hers.

And he would be no use to her as a teacher if he didn't stop this line of thought.

Her hair most definitely had to be changed.

Okay, she could do this, Maggie thought the next morning, moving into the room where Ethan and the hairstylist were waiting. It was so silly to be nervous about a simple haircut. So what if it had taken forever to grow it to just beyond her shoulders? Ethan needed her to look like someone who would be comfortable in the company of royalty, and that meant taking the scissors to her hair. So why was she dreading this moment so much?

Because when he'd kissed her yesterday in an attempt to make a point, she had gone starry-eyed like any other idiot woman, and she hadn't liked the vulnerable feeling she was left with. Her hair, riotous as it was, was a shield. It let people know ahead of time that she was not a womanly woman, so there were no surprises in store, no disappointments down the road, no chances for her to be stupidly romantic and get hurt.

Once it was lying on the floor, she would look like someone else.

"But that's the point, Maggie," she mumbled to herself. She *was* here to be transformed. And that pretty petite woman standing in the corner with Ethan was apparently the woman who was going to transform her. When she emerged from this room today, she would at least *look* different.

Maggie took a breath and looked at Ethan. Not for courage, she told herself. Just…because she knew him.

He smiled that killer smile and held out his hand. "Come meet Janette, Maggie."

Maggie placed her hand in his much larger one. His fingers closed around hers, and something terrible happened. Instant heat stroked her veins, making her tremble. When he released her almost immediately, she wanted to ask him to touch her again. She wanted to know what followed that heat. Which was just plain wrong. She tried to ignore what was happening inside her, the fact that she was acting like a ninny just because some heartbreakingly handsome man had touched her.

But when she looked at Janette, the beautiful blond woman's mouth curved up in a knowing smile.

Maggie blanched. Was she that transparent? Maybe Ethan knew, too. Maybe he'd felt her fingers trembling against his. How humiliating would that be?

Maybe it would be best to pretend nothing had happened at all. She gave the hairdresser a too hearty handshake.

"It's nice to meet you. I'm ready," she said, even though she wasn't.

Ethan raised one brow, then frowned. "Are you sure you're all right, Maggie?"

"I'm just great." She tried out a sprightly smile and purposefully sat down in the chair.

Ethan studied her for long, slow seconds. Her heart beat faster, and she hoped that he couldn't see how much he discombobulated her, darn his gorgeous body. But finally he nodded. "Janette's going to cut your hair, Maggie, but she won't do anything without first discussing what she has in mind. Right?" he asked the hairstylist.

"No surprises," Janette agreed. The woman was built like a ballerina, and she walked like one, too, as she approached Maggie, tilting her head as if to study her from all angles.

Maggie felt like a lump of bread dough, just waiting to be formed and baked into something more tasty. She tried to hold still and not squirm under the beautiful woman's scrutiny, even though squirming was something she excelled at under these kinds of circumstances.

"Let's have a look," Janette said, smoothing Maggie's hair back and lifting the mass away from her face. Surely the silence in the room went on for too long? Maybe the woman was simply going to declare there were was absolutely nothing she could do with Maggie's tangles.

Instead the woman chuckled. "Well, well, what have we here? Come look, Ethan."

Vibrations shimmered through Maggie's body as Ethan moved closer.

"It's beautiful stuff, isn't it?" he asked, and his fingers grazed a tendril of hair that had escaped its bonds.

Maggie swallowed and hoped Ethan hadn't noticed that she was barely breathing.

"Not her hair," Janette said. "Look at the curve of her neck, the shape of her head."

Don't blush. Don't blush. Maggie could tell when Ethan's gaze dropped to the exposed skin beneath her hair. She felt as if some forbidden and vulnerable part of her was on display, as if Ethan was seeing her without her clothes on. The most awful urge to pull away and hide her nakedness engulfed her.

"It's all right, Maggie," Ethan said in that low, mesmerizing voice of his. Had he read her thoughts? Had she been leaning away?

"She has a perfectly shaped head," Janette pronounced, letting Maggie's hair go. Her scruffy curls floated down around her, protecting her naked skin and lighting on her shoulders. "And the curve of her neck is delicious, don't you agree?"

Ethan didn't answer. Maggie couldn't help glancing at him from beneath her lashes, only to find him staring at her with fierce intent. Immediately his gaze shifted to Janette and he frowned, but he took a deep breath and nodded. "I see what you mean," he said tightly.

"Her hair should be short, I think," Janette was saying. "To emphasize the exquisite shape of her head. The cut will be classic, leaving nothing to the viewer's imagination. Very smooth, very sleek. A bit gamine."

Maggie tried to push away the stomach-tumbling memory of "tomboy" taunts from the days when she'd been young and her father had taken her with the boys to get her hair cut. It *is* only hair, she tried to tell herself, struggling to keep from raising her hands to feel her curls.

"I'm sure I'll look more stylish then," she said, managing what she hoped was a steady voice and a bright smile. She turned to Ethan for agreement, but he only frowned and rubbed his jaw.

He touched her hair again, so lightly that she couldn't really feel it, but she could feel *him*, the heat of his body close to hers. She breathed in his clean, male scent.

"Her hair really does have a life of its own, doesn't it?" he asked with a smile.

"Don't worry, we'll tame it," Janette announced.

"I'm sure you *could* tame it," Ethan said, his voice low and edgy.

"I'd look more civilized then, I suppose," Maggie offered, even though she quaked at the thought of the scissors.

"Less tumbled," Ethan agreed. "Less like Maggie."

Maggie nodded, and the movement brought his hand up against her skin. Sudden heat flowed through her, the decadent pleasure making her lower her lids. It was unnerving what this man could do to her, even unintentionally. She forced herself not to move and cause that sensation again.

"Don't worry, Mr. Bennington, I know what I'm doing," Janette said, and Maggie thought the woman sounded a touch amused. No doubt she was used to people anguishing over cutting their hair. Of course, it was ridiculous to worry about something as renewable as hair, anyway, Maggie supposed.

She squared her shoulders and turned toward Janette. Might as well get this over with.

"I'm ready," she said with sudden determination.

But Ethan's hand on her shoulder stopped her. "I think perhaps we should go with something a bit less drastic, Janette," Ethan said suddenly. He frowned as Janette came forward and grasped a lock of Maggie's hair as if she couldn't wait to lop it off.

"Definitely something less drastic," Ethan repeated. "I'd hate to lose all those pretty waves in her hair."

His words, his tone, commanded attention. Janette

let go of Maggie's hair and retreated a step. She opened her mouth as if she wanted to argue, then she shrugged. "I'll just start by cleaning her up," she said. "We can take it one step at a time from there."

Relief flooded though Maggie, and she looked up gratefully at Ethan. All right, maybe the plan had only been to cut her hair, but it was *her* hair. In the next few weeks she would shed so much of herself.

Maybe she wouldn't even know who she was when this was done. She might even begin to believe the charade, she thought, gazing into the mirror at Ethan after Janette had worked her magic and had gone.

"Beautiful," Ethan said. "Perfect." And he touched the long soft curls that remained after Janette had trimmed and snipped and shaped her hair. Most of the length was still there, but none of the hideous sharp edges or tangles. "What do you think, Maggie?" Ethan whispered as he gazed at the two of them framed in the mirror, his hands resting on her shoulders, her hair brushing his skin.

A silent moan ripped through her body. What she thought was that she was in big, big trouble. Ethan Bennington was touching her, and she didn't want him to stop.

"I like it. Thank you for letting me keep it," she said, but her words drew a low curse from Ethan. He moved around her and gently framed her chin with his hand.

"Maggie, I want you to promise me something. If at any time during these next few weeks you feel as if I'm pushing you too far, you're to tell me so. If anything I say or do makes you uncomfortable, I want you to say something."

"I will," she promised, but he still held her in his

grasp. His fingers were warm on her skin, and her words came out weakly.

No matter, since they'd been a lie. If she were to tell him every time he made her uncomfortable, this would never work. Ethan Bennington made her burn inside. It was simple as that, and she was just going to have to ignore the fires he lit with his touch, his voice, his smile.

Because he could never know that his touch made her ache like any other woman. She had never been like other women, and she couldn't start being that way now.

Men like Ethan had always been forbidden to women like her. They'd hurt her and left gouges in her soul, and nothing, not even a new haircut, could ever change that or make her forget the rules she lived by.

Nothing could assuage the desire she had to touch him, either, so she was just going to have to live with constant desire.

For three whole weeks.

"Maggie?"

His words made her thirst. She wanted to touch her lips to his again. "What's next?" she asked instead.

Chapter Four

This wasn't right, Ethan thought later that day after Maggie had followed him and Walter through a set of drills on walking, entering a room and the significance of titles. She had stumbled a few times, and she had to be exhausted now, but still she sat waiting for him to give her another order.

That really humbled him. Why on earth had he ever thought that this challenge might be fun? He was dealing with a human being, and turning her world upside down wasn't something he could take lightly.

This morning, when Janette had suggested cutting her hair short, Maggie's eyes had opened wide before she'd bravely forced a calm look on her face. For a minute there, he'd thought that he might have to wrestle the hairstylist to the ground. As it was, he was happy he hadn't let Janette cut Maggie's glorious hair. A short hairstyle might have been more classic, but it would have wounded her a bit.

Wounding her was the last thing he wanted. His goal

right now was to schedule a break without letting her think he was babying her. She'd already balked several times when he'd suggested she needed a rest. She'd pushed back her shoulders in a kind of "guy" gesture, one he'd just bet she'd learned from her brothers. Obviously no signs of weakness were allowed in an all-male household. So what was a desperate man supposed to do?

He sighed and slumped in his chair. "All right, I can see you're not going to cry uncle and allow me to maintain my manly dignity, are you?" he asked.

Immediately Maggie frowned. Oops. "Manly dignity" was probably laying it on too thick.

"Ethan, is something wrong?"

He shrugged. "Nothing that a little rest and fresh air won't cure."

She crossed her arms. "I can't take a rest. Just look at all this stuff." She gestured to the table where what appeared to be reams of paper were spread out. I don't have years to learn all this. Just less than three weeks."

Ethan shoved the papers aside. "Yes, well, Lionel and Walter went a bit overboard on the Internet last night. I hardly think you need to know—" he picked up a piece of paper "—the history of women's undergarments, or—" he grabbed another sheet of paper "—how to tell a man no without rendering him impotent for life." Ethan dropped the paper. "Where the hell did that come from?"

He looked up to see Maggie covering her mouth.

"What?" he asked as she giggled.

"Why do you think Walter copied that?"

"More than likely he's just worried about you, Maggie," he said softly. "A woman does need to know how to say no."

"I can take care of myself."

Sure she could. The fact that her head was drooping but she refused to stop and rest was proof of it. "I'm sure you're the Energizer bunny, Maggie, but I'm not. I'm five years older than you." Okay, that was cheap, but it was necessary.

That suspicious glint was back in her eyes. "You *are* practically a fossil," she said.

He smiled. "Ah, yes, I remember the woolly mammoths fondly."

"I see. What else do you remember, oh ancient one?" she asked with a grin.

He took a chance, got to his feet. "I remember that man does not live by lessons alone. Maggie, I need some air."

It was cheating. He'd already learned that the word *need* was her Achilles' heel.

"It's not just for me?"

And he realized it wasn't. She was a fascinating combination of bravado and naiveté, and he'd seen her eyeing his garden earlier. It would be a treat for him to observe her reactions to that special bit of Bennington Manor.

Even though the woman *did* need a break.

"I need this," he repeated, shamelessly using the ace up his sleeve. "I've arranged my schedule so that I can be away from the agency and devote my time to our project for the next few weeks, but I still have to spend part of each day closed up in my office. So, if you don't mind I'd like to take a stroll through the gardens. I haven't been there in days."

Maggie's immediate smile told him that he had made a good choice. She practically raced for the door, then caught herself and put on the brakes, her hair billowing forward over her shoulders as she stopped and it didn't.

"Sorry," she said. "I guess your average noblewoman wouldn't be stampeding through the house, would she?''

He grinned. "Well, maybe not in public, but right now we're not in public, are we?''

She frowned. "No, it doesn't work that way. I don't think it would matter whether she were in public or not. If this were real, I would have been raised to walk like a lady. Besides, doing things part of the time won't work for me. I have to get it right all the time. Otherwise I'll forget when I get excited.'' Carefully she began a sedate walk toward the door.

Her hips swung gently as she moved. Ethan's collar suddenly felt too tight. She wasn't exactly walking the way a noblewoman would walk, but whatever she was doing, it was very effective at scrambling his thoughts.

"This way," he barely managed to say, shepherding her out the door and toward the nearest of the rose gardens.

Ducking his head, he slipped under the grape arbor that served as an entrance. He held out his hand, and Maggie took it, allowing him to draw her forward.

"Oh, this is wonderful," she said, her voice nearly a whisper. "All these lawns, those crisply trimmed bushes in patterns. Roses and roses and more roses. I wish I knew more about flowers, so I could remember their names.''

"Well, you're in luck, young lady," he said, as she wandered out among the flowers, the sun glinting off the shades of red that laced her hair. "I practically hounded the gardener's footsteps when I was a boy, and he taught me as much as my parents would allow. This one is called a Heritage rose. It's English, and if you lean close, you can detect a slight lemony scent. This yellow one is Graham Thomas, a most popular English rose, and this pink, double-flowering one is called New Dawn. It was introduced in 1930 in the United States, and it was the first rose ever to hold a patent.''

She dropped to her knees in front of trellis that held up the climbing rose and smiled up at him. ''And what else do you know about roses?''

He shrugged and wished he knew more than he did. ''Oh, I know that the most popular color for roses is pink, not red, as most people think, and that most of the white, pink, yellow, peach and apricot English roses are descended from a single rose, the Constance Spry.''

''The gardener taught you all that?''

''Well, I was a bit of a pest.''

''You don't seem like a pest to me.''

''I'm not nine years old anymore.''

''You don't garden anymore?''

He chuckled. ''Well, I never did very much of that, anyway. I just asked a lot of questions. Joseph, our gardener, was very good company.''

''Didn't you have friends?''

He shrugged. ''I didn't bring them here very much.''

Maggie frowned. He had no intention of telling her that the reason he hadn't brought his friends to his house was that his parents fought constantly. And when they weren't fighting, it was because one of them was gone and the other one was usually in the bedroom with whatever sexual partner happened to be the flavor of the month.

He was just trying to figure out how to chase that concerned look from Maggie's eyes when the sound of a car heading down the long driveway distracted her.

''Who's that?'' she asked, raising her head just as Ethan turned and groaned.

Automatically Maggie surged to her feet as a sleek, red Jaguar disappeared behind the next curve.

He shook his head. "An ex-girlfriend. Ariel. She'll want to know who you are and, unlike Janette or Walter, she won't be discreet about who she tells."

"Then she can't see me. It would spoil the plan." Maggie said. The car was moving fast, so she stepped back into the shadow of the arbor.

"You head toward the house," she suggested. "If she looks over this way, I'll just—" Maggie's brow furrowed in concentration, and then she turned her back to him. Ethan started to do as she'd asked, but he stopped when he heard a ripping sound.

Turning back to her, he saw that the bottom four inches of Maggie's tunic blouse was gone. She took the scrap of blue flowered cloth and wound it round her head. Then she dropped to the ground, slid over to the nearest rose and sank her fingers into the dirt.

"Ethan!" Ariel's voice called out as she skidded to a stop in front of the house, threw open the door and moved toward him. "Ethan, hi!" She waved her hand and minced her way over to him.

Well, that had always been Ariel's way. Beautiful with an aim like a heat-seeking missile going after whatever she wanted.

"Good afternoon, Ariel," he said, trying to distract Ariel's attention away from Maggie.

He needn't have worried. The woman glanced down once at the woman playing in the dirt and roses, then immediately turned back to him.

"Ethan, it's so good to see you. It's been so-o-o long. I just had to stop and say hello. See how you are. I heard you had a lady here this morning. Anyone I know?"

Uh-oh. Potential disaster. Ethan felt a slight jolt, realizing that he and Maggie were obviously under greater scrutiny than he'd realized. He supposed the woman had been Janette. Heaven only knew how Ariel had heard. The infamous grapevine. Someone seeing Janette leaving the house. That shouldn't have been a problem. Janette didn't discuss her clients, but Ariel? He felt rather than saw Maggie stiffen on the ground beside him before she went back to her task of pretending to be patting down the earth around the rose roots.

"So you're keeping tabs on me, Ariel?" he asked.

"Of course not," she protested. "I wouldn't be so gauche, but I have an interest, a concern. We *did* date."

He nodded. "We did, but weeks ago you decided that it was best if we went our separate ways. I believe you also told me that you'd moved on and were dating someone else now."

"Yes, Edward is quite the perfect man."

Ariel lowered her lashes coquettishly, and when she glanced down, Ethan felt the breath freeze in this throat. But Ariel appeared not to even notice Maggie.

"Ariel," he said, taking her elbow to lead her away, "what exactly can I do for you?"

She resisted his tug. "I want you to come over for dinner," she blurted out suddenly. "And playtime."

Her words left him speechless. So much for Edward, the perfect man.

"Oh, I know what you're thinking," she said, her voice growing slightly shrill. "I left you. I cheated on you."

Now there was a bit of new information. Ethan thought he heard a choked gasp. He glanced out of the corner of his eye. Maggie appeared to be mangling the Graham Thomas rose. Bill, his current gardener, was going to be in tears. Ethan almost smiled as Maggie realized what she was doing and began to gently pat at the plant's base, but he quickly looked up.

"But it's different for a woman," Ariel was insisting, frowning at a space six inches to the right of Maggie's head. "I know your reputation, Ethan, and while I also know that what we had was more special than anything you'd known before, I couldn't wait for the inevitable. It's different for a man. You don't need things the way women do."

Maggie nearly jerked the rose out by its roots. She gave a light gasp and Ethan almost knelt to see what was wrong. She leaned back and waved her hand slightly, then stuck her thorn-pricked finger in her mouth.

"Then Edward was there," Ariel said, "and he was so nice, but I don't have to be exclusive with him, Ethan. You and I could still…have fun? Edward wouldn't have to know a thing."

Had he really dated this woman? Well, not exactly. He supposed he'd never known her at all.

"I'm genuinely sorry if I harmed you in some way, Ariel, but you did choose to go. So go back to Edward, now," he said wearily. "I think he'd be hurt if he knew about you coming here. It might be wise not to mention this visit to anyone."

She looked as if she was about to argue, but then she blew out a breath.

"It's the blond woman, isn't it? Who is she?"

He didn't owe her an answer, but if he didn't give one, it was only clear that she'd dig more. He didn't want her digging near Maggie.

"An old friend," he said with a shrug, which was the truth. He'd met Janette years ago.

"And I don't want lies spread about her," Ethan warned. "Furthermore, if you come here again uninvited, Edward and I will just have to have a talk." His words were harsh and if he'd had a choice, he wouldn't have said them, but there was Maggie to consider. Ariel could hurt her, and she just might choose to do that.

Ariel looked as if no one had ever told her *no* before. Maybe they hadn't. She shook her head wildly, her gaze dropped, she looked straight at and through Maggie and continued on.

"I knew you'd be like this. You always get your way, don't you? Well, I'm glad I cheated on you!" Turning on her heel, she stomped off, climbed into her car and drove away.

The air fell silent.

Ethan glanced down at Maggie. Her bright curls were tumbling out of the torn bit of cloth that covered her hair. She had a smudge of dirt on her nose, and she looked like what she was pretending to be. A very delicious gardener.

He held out one hand, but she didn't take his.

"They're dirty," she explained, looking at her own.

He clasped her hand, anyway, and pulled her up beside him.

"I'm sorry about that," he told her.

"Well, it wasn't me she was bad-mouthing," she said with a toss of her bright curls.

He chuckled. "Yes, I'd say Ariel pretty much hates my guts right now."

Maggie gave him a how-stupid-can-you-be? look. "If you called her right now, she'd hop right into your bed in a second. She's probably just mad as hell that she traded you in for Edward and burned her bridges."

For half a second Ethan felt a twinge of conscience. He hoped he hadn't hurt another woman. Part of the reason he'd chosen Ariel was because he knew she had a reputation for short-term relationships just as he did. But though she had been the one to end things, he *had* been more than ready to leave. Her pride was hurt, not her heart.

"Well, at least her coming here has accomplished one thing. We won't have to worry about her dropping in and discovering you, although...I could swear..."

"She didn't even see me, really," Maggie said, touching his arm reassuringly.

He shook his head. "Ariel has her flaws, but blindness isn't one of them."

"She didn't see me, because I wasn't important enough to notice," Maggie said. "I get this all the time in my job as a custodian. If a person is there just to do a menial job, people look right through them. They know that you're there, but you just don't count. I wasn't real for her."

Her words sent a sharp shard slicing through Ethan's thoughts. Had he been that way with his own servants? Failed to notice them? Failed to consider them real?

"You look extremely real to me," he said, and he wasn't sure if he was talking to Maggie or to himself.

"I don't think you're like Ariel," she said, and he knew that she'd guessed at his train of thought. "You remember your gardener's name, don't you? The one who taught you so much?"

He shrugged. "That's too easy. Joseph was Bill's father. Bill's the gardener here now," he explained.

"And I'll bet you talk to him the way you talked to Joseph. And the way you talk to Walter."

"Not always."

She shrugged. "Sometimes servants—or custodians—have to be invisible. It's part of the job description. We all know and respect that. It's only at times like this, when someone discusses things that should be private in front of us, that we know we're not real to that person. You wouldn't do that."

He smiled and shook his head. "Seems to me I just did."

She laughed then, a rich, low laugh. "But you knew I was there. I could tell you didn't want to say those things in front of me. You kept glancing my way. I could feel it."

He stared down at her smiling countenance, then reached out and freed her hair from the cloth that held it in place. Her curls swung free, brushing her shoulders.

"Do you think Bill will forgive me for touching his prize rosebush?" she asked suddenly. "I'm afraid I may have harmed it with all that patting and digging."

Ethan looked at the plant, which was still standing tall and proud. "We'll go tell him that one of his babies needs some TLC. He'll forgive you when he sees how much you like his roses. And then we'll have some lunch. You're going to need sustenance."

"You have work for me to do?"

"You might say that."

"What kind?"

He smiled, reached out and touched the frayed edge of her blouse where she had ripped it.

"You need a new blouse."

"That wasn't an answer."

"Ah, but it was, Maggie. It was."

And he grinned and took her hand, leading her to the house.

Chapter Five

There was no one else in the store. That was what Maggie couldn't get out of her mind the next morning as she watched Ethan direct the saleswoman to bring him various articles of clothing. The lady had just gone off in search of a gown in emerald green when Maggie rose on her toes beside him.

"Where are all the other people?" she whispered. "The customers? The salespeople?"

Ethan smiled down at her and leaned close, his lips near her ear. "I'm afraid there are no other people. Just you and me and Estelle." His warm breath caressed her skin; his low voice was achingly sexy.

Maggie almost moved closer, then caught herself and took a step back. "How can that be?"

He tilted his head, a not-so-innocent look of innocence in his eyes. "We needed privacy, Estelle was glad to close her shop for 'inventory' and oblige us."

"And she doesn't mind the lost business today?" Maggie's brow furrowed as she studied the situation.

"It doesn't seem so. She's been very…pleasant so far."

And suddenly Maggie got it. The petite and exquisitely coifed gray-haired woman had been more than pleasant. She had beamed, she had been ecstatic at the prospect of dressing "Ethan's lady." She had agreed that she understood that this was a private affair he and Maggie were having.

"You paid her to close her store so that no one would see us here, didn't you?" Maggie asked.

"It seemed best," he agreed with an innocent air.

And suddenly she couldn't help laughing. "You amaze me, do you know that? It must have cost you a fortune to shut down a store for hours so that no one would see us and recognize me later, and yet you seem completely unconcerned."

He shrugged. "It's not that big a deal."

Maybe for him it wasn't, but she wasn't sure she bought into that. Even a rich man didn't go this far. Usually.

"It's very important to you that you win Lionel's trust and his business, isn't it?"

"My father almost buried the agency by being greedy and dishonest with customers. Rebuilding trust and reestablishing my honor is very important to me."

"And if I do this right, Lionel will help you and that will make a difference."

"Lionel doesn't make foolish business decisions. He doesn't hire untrustworthy firms."

"Well then," Maggie said, holding her arms out her side as she heard Estelle calling out from the stockroom. "What are we waiting for? Dress me, Ethan."

For half a second Ethan froze. His silver eyes stared into hers intensely. Then he raised one brow.

"With pleasure," he said, his low voice swirling about her.

And suddenly Maggie felt uncertain. "I'm not very good at choosing clothes." Panic almost overtook her as Estelle approached with an armload of dresses.

Ethan stepped behind Maggie. He leaned down and whispered into her hair, "Just follow my lead. I promise not to dress you in anything that would embarrass you."

And he didn't. For the next hour Ethan chose outfit after outfit. He shook his head at some things Estelle brought, nodded at others. His taste was impeccable, Maggie had to agree as she was marched off to the dressing room time after time, as Estelle tucked and pinned and discussed Maggie with Ethan.

"She has a nice bosom," Estelle said, matter-of-factly, and Maggie was sure she turned as red as Estelle's fingernails.

"Indeed, she does," Ethan said with a wink at Maggie.

"And a tiny waist," Estelle added.

"I've noticed," Ethan agreed, and Maggie's pulse lurched.

Estelle seemed to take Ethan's supposed knowledge of Maggie's body for granted, and Maggie wondered how many women he'd brought here. "And her derriere—" Estelle began, but Maggie let out a whoop.

"Oops, sorry, I must have gotten stuck with a pin," she said, whirling around so that Ethan's eyes wouldn't shift to her caboose. She was already squirming enough beneath the man's attentions. Honestly, just having this man look at her was almost as intimate as having some men actually reach out and touch. Those lazy silver eyes of his didn't miss a thing. She was pretty darn sure that he could mentally undress a woman without even trying.

When she looked up, flushed and flustered, Ethan was grinning at her, his dimples evident. "You have a beautiful posterior, Ms. Todd," he said, bowing to kiss her hand.

She couldn't help smiling at that. It was so obvious that he had understood her discomfort and attempted to tease her out of her distress.

"Well, I'm just not used to having my body parts examined so closely," she said with a self-conscious shrug.

"Oh, but the men must adore your body," Estelle said in a shocked voice.

Maggie felt warmth creeping up her chest. "Actually, men generally don't think of me that way. Or maybe some of them do, but they just want to grab, not talk about it. Not that I mind. The last thing I want in my life is a man."

She tried not to look at Ethan after she'd let that gaffe slip out about being grabbed, but she couldn't help it. There was just something about him that demanded she look at him.

When she did, she saw that Ethan's eyes had turned cold.

"I promise you, Maggie, when you dance at the ball in this gown," he said, fingering the emerald-green silk dress he and Estelle had decided on, "there will be no men grabbing you. And every man will want to get close enough to compliment you."

She didn't contradict him. He just didn't understand that other men didn't see her the way he saw women, as fragile, beautiful beings. "If it doesn't happen," she continued before he could rush in with some well-meaning compliment. "That's fine. I told you before, I'm used to dealing with men."

"Obviously the wrong kind of men," he insisted, but before she could say anything else, he turned to Estelle.

"And now, we move down her body to her feet, I think."

"Oh, yes, shoes are so important," Estelle agreed.

"Uh-oh," Maggie said.

Estelle and Ethan both turned toward her.

"I think you should know that I am an absolute klutz if we're talking something without rubber soles," Maggie told them.

Estelle looked horrified. Ethan looked amused.

"We'll see," he said, and for the next forty-five minutes Maggie tried on shoes. She hadn't been lying about her lack of balance in anything other than practical shoes, but still she couldn't help wishing she were more graceful when Estelle brought out a pair of dainty, silvery four-inch heels. With slender straps that crisscrossed the toes and one tiny bit of leather to keep them on her ankles they were the most delicate, beautiful shoes Maggie had ever seen. She was almost afraid to even look at them.

Carefully slipping them on, she unsteadily rose to her feet. For half a second, she was almost balanced, almost steady. Then everything happened at once. Maggie's ankles, too used to sturdier footgear, wobbled. Reaching out for purchase, she slipped and toppled over right into Ethan's arms.

He caught her, slipping his arm around her waist and steadying her. She tried to ignore the feel of his fingers splayed against her side. She wondered how many women had felt his touch, how many women he'd *cho-*

sen to hold close, and not in a situation like this where he was simply being considerate.

"These shoes are so beautiful, but they aren't very practical for someone like me, are they?" she asked sadly, softly, turning to face him and finding him much closer than she knew how to deal with. "I don't think I could ever walk in them." Maggie barely managed to squeeze the words from her mouth. Ethan was so alarmingly, so mesmerizingly close. The situation with the beautiful shoes, and with the beautiful man was so pointless, so clearly forbidden to her, that she felt suddenly small and inadequate and totally lacking in the kinds of things that made most women feel like women.

"A pity about the shoes," Estelle said, unboxing a pair of much lower pumps. "Heels do wonders for a woman's legs."

"Maggie's legs don't need any enhancing," Ethan said, as he helped Maggie back into her chair and she gave a tiny sigh as she removed the beautiful shoes.

In the end they settled on a combination of stylish low-heeled pumps as well as several pairs of flats for those days when she was just wandering Ethan's mansion on her own.

"It's a good thing you have a big house," Maggie told Ethan as they left the store, leaving their packages to be delivered later. "I couldn't even fit all of those clothes into my tiny apartment. I'm not really sure why I needed so much, anyway. You said I only needed to be onstage for one night."

Ethan only smiled. "You'll need to be comfortable in your new clothes by the time that day rolls around. Practice begins today, Maggie."

And suddenly she remembered just what a monumental task she had to look forward to. It had been fun trying on clothes with only Ethan and Estelle to notice if she tugged at her skirt or teetered even on two-inch heels, but once she hit the big time, she had to do everything perfectly.

Maggie's hands felt suddenly cold. Already she was worrying about the consequences of failing Ethan.

When they arrived back at the house, Ethan let out a groan. Bounding toward them with the speed of a cheetah was a big, black anvil-headed dog, his tongue hanging out, his intense forward movement practically spinning him head over heels several times. His large clumsy paws slapped at the earth as he bounded forward, bent on reaching them with all possible speed.

Instinctively Ethan stepped in front of Maggie.

"Stay, Poe," he bellowed, and the huge dog put on the brakes, skidding, his bottom dragging the grass and slowing him to a stop three feet in front of Ethan. The dog whimpered and tilted his big head in supplication.

"Where's Walter?" Ethan asked more to himself than to anyone. Of course, he knew the answer. He had given Walter the afternoon off, and the afternoon had not ended.

"Oh, he's so sweet," Maggie said, rushing forward as if the dog were the size of a mouse. "Whose is he?"

"He's—" *Walter's* Ethan had almost said, before he remembered. "He's mine, but Walter keeps him at his cottage. Poe...well, let's just say that Poe and I didn't meet by choice. He was a present from a former...friend."

Maggie scratched behind the dog's ears and smiled down at the look of ecstasy on Poe's face. "One of your debutante girlfriends gave you a homely dog the size of a tank?"

Ethan couldn't help chuckling himself. "Well, he

was a puppy when he arrived. Not nearly so mammoth.''

She nodded. ''If he's yours, why does Walter keep him?''

He didn't answer right away. He wasn't sure what to say.

He looked down to find Maggie studying him intently. ''Does he bring back bad memories of the relationship?'' Then she clapped her hand over her mouth. ''I can't believe I asked something so definitely not my business.''

''Maggie, forget it. It's nothing like that. I'm just— Well, dogs and I don't seem to get along. I never had one as a kid, and I just— Well, I'm just not a natural with animals.''

''That's okay, you don't have to explain. Lots of people feel that way. At my house, we always had pets. When my parents adopted me, I was like another addition to the menagerie. They had three sons of their own, two dogs, two cats, a hamster, a bird and a fish, but something was still missing, my mother said. At least that's what my father told me. I never knew either of my mothers. The first one—well, I don't know about her at all, and the other one, my dad's wife, she died when I was very little. Anyway, I was supposed to finish things off and make the family complete. Only my uncle and his wife died, and Will came to live with us, too. The Todds have a great tolerance for noise and mayhem,'' she finished with a smile. ''We're all kind of rough and rowdy. A dog like Poe would be right at home there, even if most *people* wouldn't.''

Ethan couldn't help wondering again how Maggie felt about this whole scenario. She obviously came from a big, happy family, people who loved her.

"How does your family feel about all this?" he asked suddenly, gesturing around him.

"You mean about my being here?"

He nodded.

"Well, they don't really know anything except that I'm working up north." She concentrated on stroking Poe's fur.

"Maggie," he drawled.

"Well," she said defensively. "I wanted to make sure your secret didn't get out. Besides, my father and my brothers are just a little protective. We've had 'incidents' when things didn't work out between me and my dates, and when my former fiancé decided I really wasn't what he wanted in a life partner, I thought I was going to have to pull out a baseball bat and defend him from my family. I just didn't want any of them getting upset when I came here of my own free will."

"They'll worry, Maggie."

"They'll worry more if they know I'm living with a man. Besides, as I told you, I'm an adult. I can handle things myself."

But three hours later Ethan wasn't so sure. They sat at a table, a stack of photos in the center. It was time to begin the task they'd set out to do.

"So I'm to be the great-great-granddaughter of the Duke of Tarrington. Does that mean I have to pretend to be a duchess or something like that?" She sounded tremendously worried.

Ethan took her very soft, very cold hand in his. Gently he folded his fingers about hers, trying to warm her while struggling to ignore the feel of her skin against his.

He smiled. "Ah, that's the beauty of being a duke's great-great-granddaughter. You don't have a title unless you marry a man with his own title. You get the prestige without having to have everyone struggle to remember what to call you.''

Maggie nodded tightly. ''Well, that's good. It's one less thing I have to pretend about.'' And he knew then that she was more stressed than she usually would admit to. She would experience more distress in the weeks to come. But before he could follow that thought, she reached for the stack of photos.

''Okay, let's begin,'' she said, and she looked up at him, determination in the stubborn set of her lovely chin and in the bold look in her brown eyes.

''You're still with me?'' he asked softly.

Her chin rose higher. ''I gave my word, and I took your money. This is for the children of Safe House and for your grandfather. It's important, and it really isn't hurting anyone. It's kind of like Halloween, only we're the only ones who'll know I'm not for real.''

Ethan reached out and tucked one finger beneath that firm little chin. ''You're very much for real, Maggie. Thank you.''

But his touch and his words sent a tiny tremor through her. A flicker of panic flitted through her eyes, and he felt her swallow nervously.

Instantly he released her. He turned to the photos. ''These are the people who'll be at the party. Lionel and I have chosen them by their pedigrees. Many of them have old money. Those who don't have power.'' He knew that that wasn't what Maggie needed to hear in order to stay calm, but she needed to be privy to the truth. Still…

''They're rich and powerful, but rich and powerful people are still just people, Maggie. No better or worse than you. And all you have to do is convince them that you're charming, that you're elegant, that you're one of them.''

She opened her mouth, then quickly shut it, her teeth clicking with the force of her action. "Tell me about this one."

"Helen Flora," he said with a smile. "Aged somewhere over seventy, she won't say how much. Very flowery like her name, very dreamy. Her husband died twenty years ago. She lives for parties, she's easy to please. Just look demure and smile at her stories even if she tells them twenty times over."

Maggie nodded. She scribbled some notes on a pad he gave her. "And this one?" she asked.

It went on. Things were going well, until he came to the photo he'd been dreading, the woman Lionel had insisted on. "Sylvia Montcrief," he offered. "Has everything, knows everyone, makes it her business to grill each newcomer. She'll be difficult to fool and she'll be looking for missteps."

"Because she suspects us?"

Ethan grimaced. "Sylvia suspects everyone she meets. She's very protective of her social circles, and she doesn't want anyone entering it who isn't legit. Perhaps it comes from spending so many seasons in Palm Beach, where pretending to be royalty or members of the elite set is an occupation for some. She claims she can spot an interloper from twenty paces."

The silence was deadening. When he turned to look at Maggie, she had closed her eyes and she was taking a deep breath. Slowly she opened her eyes. "I guess I'll just have to put on a really good show and win the costume contest," she said, her voice somewhat shaky.

He frowned, confused.

"You know, the Halloween thing," she said. "In our neighborhood we would all trick-or-treat and then, to make it last a little longer, we'd ask all our neighbors to vote on the best costume they'd seen. Then we'd have a party, crown the winner, dunk for apples until we were all choking from laughing and swallowing too much water, and then when the adults decided we'd waited long enough, we'd all fall on our bags of candy. A great holiday, Halloween, isn't it?''

"I'm sure it is," Ethan agreed noncommittally.

But Maggie was looking just as suspicious as Sylvia Montcrief ever had. She gazed up into his eyes as if searching for something she'd lost there.

"What?" he finally asked.

"You say that as if you never went trick-or-treating," she said.

"My parents considered it begging," he finally admitted.

A look of sudden and sweet sadness colored her brown eyes and she touched his arm. "I'm sorry."

But he shook his head and smiled. "You don't miss what you never had, Maggie."

"No, I guess you don't." And Ethan realized just how much distance separated them. Their life experiences in the past and those in the future were and would always be so very different. Only for this short time would they come together.

"We don't have much time." He said the words aloud.

"I know." Her voice was filled with dread, and he knew that they were talking about different things. She was thinking of how much she had to learn in so little time. He was thinking that he'd never had any opportunity to cross paths with someone like Maggie and probably wouldn't again. But she was right. He needed to concentrate on the task at hand.

So he'd spent the rest of the afternoon teaching Maggie the ins and outs of who was who in local society, giving her pointers on how to handle small talk with some of the more self-important people she would no doubt be forced to interact with at the party. Maggie had shown an astonishing capacity for remembering names and matching them to the photos he showed her, but once when he'd glanced away, he'd looked back to find an expression of stark terror in her eyes. Quickly she'd tried to mask it...and failed.

"I am going to completely mangle this," she said, her voice coming out soft and strangled.

Ethan slid his chair closer. He took her cold hand and gently massaged her fingers. He leaned close and whispered near her ear. "You're the best pupil I've ever had."

She managed to laugh at that, but only for a second. "Oh no, you don't," she said. "You're not going to convince me that you've done this before. No one would be insane enough to do this twice. Would they?" she asked, looking up at him with those big golden-brown eyes.

He wanted to tell her that he'd waltzed a million women through this if it would make things easier for her, but something about those oh-so-perceptive brown eyes stopped him.

"You're the only one," he whispered.

She closed her eyes.

"Lean on me, Maggie. I won't let you fall."

"That's not what I'm worried about," she said. "I'm the one who might let you fall."

"You won't. You couldn't. This isn't that important," he assured her.

But he could tell that she didn't believe him, and how could he blame her? She held in her hands the capacity to give back to him something he'd lost. The business was all tied up with his love for his grandfather and his loss. This business was all he'd ever had that he felt was really a part of him and not some part of his parents' twisted relationship. He couldn't deny that he burned to put things right, that he needed to make his own mark in the world and set out in a new direction. He needed Maggie to do that, but...

"I'll protect you from Sylvia as much as I can," he promised fiercely.

She shook her head. "My father always told me that I'd have to stand on my own two feet, that I couldn't rely on the boys and him to always be there, as much as they wanted to. It's the only way I can live and survive. Sometimes they're there for me, but sometimes they can't be. If I don't know how to get by on my own, I'll go under when things get tough. I have to be able to do this on my own, Ethan—Sylvia Montcrief and all. I have to learn."

Maybe so, but there was doubt in her voice. Maybe what he had asked Maggie to do for him was going to be the one thing he should never have asked of her. She'd been hurt before. If he added to that in any way, he was no kind of man at all.

But there was no going back now. Maggie herself needed to go forward and succeed. He feared they were both on a path leading to regret.

He had set the scene and started the wheels turning. He'd drawn Maggie in against her will, and now... heaven help him if he hurt her. And he had the terrible feeling that, blunt and full of bluster and bravado as she appeared, Maggie Todd might be the most fragile blossom of a woman he'd ever known.

It was a thought that stayed with him through the day, all through dinner, when he noticed the gathering shadows beneath her eyes and the hint of fatigue that crept into her voice, which she kept pushing away by grasping the table and shaking her head, forcing a smile.

Finally he couldn't let her struggle any longer.

"To bed, my lady," he said, and she looked up at him then, wide-eyed and confused, her eyes soft and luminous, her lips even softer, full and pink.

He nearly groaned with frustration.

"You need your sleep," he clarified. "We've a long day ahead of us tomorrow."

She blinked, looked away and gave him a tight nod, clearly embarrassed at what she'd thought for a second. But she quickly recovered, pasting on an overly bright smile.

"You don't have to worry about me, Ethan," she assured him. "I'll be fine."

But she stumbled slightly as she neared the stairs. She *was* tired. He'd pushed her too hard today. He hoped she would sleep a long and dreamless and reviving sleep. He promised himself that he would watch her more closely the next day, be more careful of her, now that he was learning her limitations.

Hours later, long after the time when the house should have been completely still and Maggie should have been sleeping for hours, Ethan glanced out the window. There, on the rolling expanse of the east lawn, hidden from view of the driveway, he saw her. Her hair was loose, her feet were bare, she was wearing ripped jeans and a white sleeveless blouse that had seen many years of wear. She was romping on the grass with Poe, having him fetch a stick, then patting him and rolling with him when he caught it. Her hair was wild, her limbs were loose. She looked nothing like a noble-woman, much more like a woman made to grace a man's bed than his table.

For the first time all day she looked relaxed and free.

Ethan wondered if he had done the right thing in allowing Lionel to choose Maggie. Would they be able to pull this off? And would Maggie still be Maggie when he was done with her?

He wondered something else, too. How was he going to keep himself from throwing open the door and joining her on the lawn? It seemed like an unimportant question, but he knew it was not. Because right now what he wanted to do more than anything was to finish what he'd started when he'd kissed her that first day.

He wanted to taste Maggie's lips once again. He wanted to taste all of her. It was a hunger, deep and irrationally strong. For Maggie's sake, he hoped he could hold it at bay.

At that moment, she looked up. Her startled eyes stared into his, and then she smiled. The impact of her expression stole the breath from Ethan's lungs. Naked beauty stretched out on his lawn, smiling at him invitingly.

He longed to do nothing more than to smile back, take the stairs three at a time and run out on the lawn to experience that smile at close range.

And if he did?

He would be worse than Poe, knocking her to the ground, straining to be close to her, willing to take anything she could give.

He would be worse, because Poe was a dog. Selfishness was expected. And what Poe wanted was simple. A chance to romp, some basic affection.

What *he* wanted was so much more dangerous. Maggie naked and moaning beneath him. Maggie waking in the morning to realize he'd used her far worse than he'd ever meant to as a result of their simple transaction at the auction. If he didn't guard his actions, he would take all her sweetness, steal all her warmth, but he had absolutely nothing to offer in return.

Ethan stepped back from the window. He didn't allow himself to go near the east lawn.

Chapter Six

The night had been long and restless, and yet Maggie still woke too early the next morning. A sense of dread filled her. She was hard-pressed not to run to her mirror to see if any of Ethan's miraculous transformation had taken place.

"Oh, sure, like that would happen overnight," she mumbled to herself. And if she looked in the mirror, what would she see?

Same old rough-edged Maggie.

Except she wasn't the same. There was a nervousness about her, an edgy sense of fear and frustration.

No question about the reason why. It was Ethan. As huge as this house was, his presence filled it. And as much as she tried to avoid thinking of him, she couldn't seem to manage it. It wasn't just the fact that she was afraid of failing him, either, even though she was. After yesterday afternoon, she knew just how many people she was going to have to fool. And they weren't just nameless, faceless entities anymore, either. They had names, they had pedigrees, and she knew they would see right through her act. She was going to let Ethan down.

Today that mattered more than it had yesterday. Now she knew something about him. She knew that his childhood hadn't been idyllic and that he didn't want love. She knew that he felt uncomfortable because a big, needy dog had come into his life.

The man was just too much on her mind. Last night, on the lawn with Poe, she'd promptly forgotten everything Ethan had taught her and behaved just like the wild tomboy she always had been. Torn jeans. No self-control. And when she'd looked up to find Ethan staring out the window at her, she'd been shocked at the warmth that had flooded her body. She'd wanted nothing more than to have him with her, tumbling on the grass. She'd almost called out loud to invite him down, just before she'd realized that yelling through the night was probably not the way a noblewoman would conduct herself.

No matter. Ethan had gazed down at her and Poe for a few seconds. Then he'd promptly closed himself off.

"Well, what should he have done? Come rolling around on the dirty ground with you and Poe?" she asked herself with disgust. "The man is a Bennington, woman. A member of a family that's been contributing to the society page for over a hundred years. What would his grandfather say if Ethan began consorting with a woman who fixes toilets and sweeps floors?"

She shut her eyes to close off the image of Alexander Bennington shaking his head sadly at his grandson, but it didn't work. She needed something to do with her hands and her mind.

As she paced her room, her gaze lit on the crystal doorknob. Beautiful, but a bit loose. Nothing much really, but suddenly she felt a sense of relief. Running to the closet where she'd left her bag, she ferreted out the tiny tool kit she carried with her everywhere. An odd habit to be sure, but it had come in handy over the years, and it was eminently more practical for a woman like herself than a makeup kit.

Kneeling before the door, she tightened the screws that held the delicate doorknob in place. Then she quietly slipped out the door and moved down the hall, testing and adjusting the rest of the doorknobs. She'd brought a small pad of paper and a pencil with her and what she couldn't fix with the tools and supplies she had, she wrote down on her paper. Not that there was much to do, but even a well-run house like Ethan's could use a repair here and there. A sense of purpose zinged through Maggie's body, a sense of the world righting itself.

She was kneeling in front of the door to the library when a sudden noise sent her spinning around.

"Maggie, are you all right?"

Maggie froze as if she'd been caught looking into Ethan's closet. She looked up and saw that he was halfway down the staircase. His hair was delightfully mussed, his white shirt wasn't completely buttoned. He looked…sinful. He looked like everything every woman in the world wanted in her bed.

Maggie was suddenly aware that she was wearing nothing but a shortie pair of pajamas that had eye-popping electric blue, red and green frogs dancing around on a bright yellow background. She was also aware she had been caught on her knees with a screwdriver in her hand. And most important, she was aware that she had obviously awakened Ethan with her early-morning prowling.

"Oh no, I'm so sorry," she whispered. "It's too early, isn't it? I didn't mean to be so noisy."

He continued moving down the stairs. "You

weren't. I just knew someone was up, and Walter never shows up until seven.''

''Oh, my, then you can't even have coffee. I'll make some.'' Maggie pivoted in the direction of the kitchen.

But by then Ethan had made it down the stairs, and he laid a hand on her arm to stop her mad rush from the hallway.

''Maggie, don't. There's no need for that. While you're here, this is your home. You don't have to apologize for roaming the house early or for making noise, and you certainly don't have to cook for me.''

''Even if it makes me feel better?''

He grinned. ''How about I make *you* coffee?''

She couldn't keep the startled look from her eyes.

Ethan laughed. ''You're right, I don't guarantee the quality, but I've tried it a time or two. Are you brave enough to try my coffee, my lady?''

She put down her screwdriver and her pad of paper and crossed her arms. ''I have the distinct impression that you're trying to manipulate me.''

''I'm just trying to stress that we're a team,'' he said, ''partners in this little adventure we're on. We're in this together, and if we're going to risk Walter's ire by messing in his kitchen, then we're going to share the danger.''

She raised one brow. ''Walter doesn't seem like the type to throw a temper tantrum.''

''There's more to Walter than meets the eye. Obviously more to you, too. Mind if I ask what you were doing?''

A trickle of guilt crept in.

''Fixing a few things? Making a list of things I could repair while I'm here? Oh, I guess I shouldn't be doing this, should I? I'm supposed to be learning debutante stuff, not rushing around nosing into other people's plumbing and electrical problems, aren't I?'' She bit her lip and tried to look just a bit more sophisticated, as sophisticated as was possible given the screaming color of her frog pajamas.

Ethan reached out and picked up her nearly empty pad. He studied the columns she'd made where she'd intended to put the most pressing jobs, the ones that could wait another week, the ones that were long-term.

"You enjoy fixing things, don't you?" he asked, a pained look in his eyes.

She wanted to say no, that it wasn't important at all. "Yes," she agreed. "It's so…basic, and I'm good at it."

"Then I'll make the coffee, you finish your list, but…"

Her head came up at the tone of his voice. She waited for him to finish his thought, but he seemed to have forgotten that he was speaking. His gaze lit on her midsection. It traveled down to the tops of her thighs where fabric became bare skin. Suddenly he jerked his head up as if someone had slugged him.

"Ethan?"

He looked at her. For two seconds she thought he wasn't even going to speak. Finally he shook his head as if to clear it. "Nice pajamas," he said.

It was the last thing she'd expected him to say. She looked down at herself, and the reds, greens and blues seemed brighter than ever. She wondered if his eyes were hurting. Probably all the women he knew wore black, even to bed. Or maybe they wore nothing, she thought, swallowing hard, which would still be more tasteful than what she had on. "I guess they *are* a little loud, aren't they?"

He cleared his throat and began to button his shirt. "They're cute. You look pretty in them. Let me get you a robe," he said, and Maggie finally "got it" as heat zipped up and down her body.

What should have been obvious to an ordinary woman had flown right past her. She'd been wearing these pajamas forever. They were like old, comfortable friends. But now she suddenly realized just how much of her legs were visible. She had an urge to tug down the legs of her pajama bottoms, but there was almost nothing to tug on. No doubt about it, she'd made another gaffe. What self-respecting nobleman's great-great-granddaughter would wear something like this?

"I'll just go change," she said, uneasily, sliding toward her room. "I guess I wasn't thinking. I—"

He shook his head. "Don't do that. You thought you were alone. I'm not going to dictate what you wear to bed, Maggie."

But his voice was a little strained as he spoke, his eyes a little dark. She wondered if that was disapproval in his eyes. Or disappointment. He was probably thinking that he was going to have to work even harder than he'd thought at first if he was going to get her up to speed.

"No problem. I'll wear them when I get home again," she said. "For now I've got all those nice froufrou things you bought me. I probably should start taking things more seriously, really getting into character. Can't do that wearing glow-in-the-dark frogs. I just didn't think last night. I just grabbed for the most comfortable thing, and so…" She held out her hands and looked down at the frogs on her chest. "Anyway, tonight I promise I'll wear something more proper, more plain, something longer and more—"

"Stuffy?" he asked with a smile.

"That wasn't what I meant to say." She shook her head vehemently, even though she *had* been thinking something along those lines. She hated the high necks and leg-choking long skirts of the gowns in her room, but if that was what the great-great-granddaughter of a duke would wear, she could do that. "I was going to say, um, nice," she finished lamely.

Ethan chuckled. "Nice try, Maggie. You really don't

have to wear the gowns if they don't suit you. I doubt we'll be doing much entertaining in the middle of the night. With Walter in his cottage, we're alone after the sun goes down. You're safe from prying eyes.'' But he looked down at her legs again and took a deep breath, his mouth tightening. ''I'll get you a robe,'' he said again.

''You already did,'' she reminded him. ''Yesterday at Estelle's. It's white satin. I'll wear it.'' And she was sure she didn't imagine the relief in his eyes. He didn't like her near nakedness. She wondered if he thought her wanton, and she realized that she felt slightly wanton standing here in front of him half-dressed. Suddenly she felt shy.

''I think I *will* get dressed, though,'' she said suddenly, turning toward her room.

''Maggie?''

She turned and looked at him.

''This is hard enough for you,'' he said. ''Wear what you want to bed. I'm sorry if I made you feel uncomfortable, and yes, for the record, I was looking at your legs. It was unforgivable, and it was not your fault. I'll try to keep my eyes where they belong from now on.''

And suddenly she knew that this whole situation wasn't easy for him, either. He was trying to save his business, but she would bet he would have chosen some other method if he'd had a choice. That thought freed her somewhat.

Maggie smiled. She planted her hands on her hips. Then she wrinkled her nose. ''Mr. Bennington,'' she said in as haughty a manner as she could muster, ''I'll have you know that my great-great-grandfather was the Duke of Tarrington, and he would definitely have held me responsible for keeping my legs decently covered. The frogs will keep. From now on I'm a white satin lady. So you'd better look fast, because you won't see these legs again.''

A slow, lazy smile transformed his face. "Thank you, I will take one last peek," he teased. And he trained his gaze on her ankles and traveled upward to the curve of her calf, the bend of her knee, the length of her thigh.

Maggie shrieked and ran toward her room.

"You win, you win, I'm sorry I woke you, and I'm sorry I wore these awful pajamas."

His laugh followed her down the hall. "Don't be gone long, Maggie. I'll have coffee in a minute. And Maggie?"

She peeked around the door.

He nodded toward where she had left her tools and her pad. "As long as you're there for me when I need you, go ahead and do what you have to in order to relieve the tension the rest of the time. If that means dancing with my dog or pounding nails or sleeping with frogs, I'll understand."

A short time later, with Ethan's terrible coffee as fuel, Ethan planned the day's lessons. Maggie continued with her list, but this time they were more companionable. She guessed she'd just needed time to really commit herself to being a nobleman's descendant, and now she had.

As she scribbled quietly, Ethan looked up. "If you're going to repair things, I'm going to pay you."

"The nobility does not work for hire," she said, beginning to enjoy her role. She and her brothers used to make up wild stories for each other.

"The nobility doesn't know which end of a pipe wrench is up. And neither do I," Ethan explained, "but I know I don't take services I didn't pay for."

"You paid. A lot."

"Not to you."

"Yes. To me. I've volunteered the next few weeks away. And the kids at Safe House mean a lot to me.

They're kids who need a chance. Like orphans. Like I did. You gave them one.''

"I wasn't thinking of them at the time."

"Doesn't matter. It all ends up the same."

He didn't say anything for a minute, but she knew he still watched her. It was too difficult to breathe. The knee-length black skirt she'd chosen didn't change the fact that twenty minutes earlier, she'd been all naked legs, and that Ethan had looked his fill. Joking, of course. He had plenty of women willing to crawl to him, according to the gossip. And Ariel. And she had plenty of proof that she wasn't any man's fantasy, but still her throat felt tight.

She needed not to think about him. She scribbled madly, not even sure what all she was writing down, and when she finally pushed down on her pen so hard that she ripped the paper, she looked up to find Ethan watching her.

"You appear to have made quite a list," he said.

She let her gaze slide away from his. Heaven only knew what was on the list. Hopefully not a description of Ethan's eyes—or his bare chest the way it had looked this morning.

She shrugged. "Just little things. They won't take too much time."

"That's good, then. The next few weeks may be tense.

"You do what you want to do, but don't feel that I expect you to take on chores. I don't want you wearing yourself out trying to do the work of two people."

She wanted to protest, to tell him she could do it all. But could she? She didn't have a clue what kinds of things Ethan still had to teach her, but she doubted she could learn her "noblewoman" lessons as quickly as she'd learned to wield a drill. Maybe it was best to wait, see how things went, but—

"I promise I'll pace myself," she agreed. "But you

should understand that it's important that I carry my weight.''

She shifted from one foot to another then, and Ethan's gaze dropped to her slender body.

''Not a lot of weight,'' he mused, but his voice was low. She didn't feel insulted the way she did when most men questioned her abilities.

''Lots of things don't need heft,'' she said softly. ''Just patience and a careful examination of the situation.''

He stared down into her eyes, his own clear and deep and mesmerizing. ''You're right. It's always important to be aware of every angle of every situation.''

And he was close enough that Maggie was sure he could hear her heart thundering, that he could feel how shaky and soft and whimpery her breath was as it left her body. She needed to get control of her self, to stop acting like this around him every time he came within three feet of her.

She took a deep breath and raised her chin.

''A noblewoman is always aware of every angle and always prepared,'' she said, hoping she sounded aristocratic enough, uninvolved enough.

Ethan blinked. He gazed at her with those deep silver eyes, and every coherent thought she held fled.

''That sounded dumb, didn't it?'' she asked.

He chuckled. ''You don't know just how authentic that played. You're very good at this pretending game, Maggie.''

''This could be fun, now that I'm settling in,'' she said.

''It could,'' he agreed, in that deep voice that would have had any normal woman begging him to move closer, to kiss her. ''As long as we both know we're pretending. We're going to be friends, Maggie. We're going to be close, but don't ever pretend that I'm something I'm not. I'm a good businessman, but I'm not a good man. Ariel was right to leave me when she did.''

''Ariel was—she was a cheater,'' Maggie said with some heat, but when Ethan chuckled at her vehemence and shook his head sadly, Maggie thought that she felt a little sorry for Ariel. The woman had had this man and known that she was going to lose him.

That thought alone could lead a woman to do crazy things.

Maggie decided then and there that she was going to do her best for Ethan, but she hoped against hope that she didn't do anything crazy, and she was afraid that she already had.

Because when Ethan had moved close a moment ago, it had taken all she had not to loop her arms around his neck and drag his lips to hers, and that would have been a disaster. She'd been like Ariel before. She'd lived with the knowledge that a man didn't want her, and she didn't want to ever go there again.

But by all that was noble, she wanted to feel the heat of Ethan's mouth on hers again. Too bad that part of the pretending was over.

Chapter Seven

She was absolutely amazing to watch, Ethan thought six days later, studying Maggie as she practically ran the perimeter of his study balancing a book on her head.

"How am I doing?" she asked, as she passed him for the third time, her auburn curls breezing out behind her, her soft blue skirt pressing against her legs.

A low chuckle escaped him. "If you'd just put it in low gear, you'd be absolutely perfect."

His words brought her to an abrupt stop. "Uh-oh, I'm rushing again, aren't I? Why didn't you tell me?" she asked.

He took the book she'd caught in her hand. "I just did. And don't be so hard on yourself. It's just a little thing. You're almost there. You have the most amazing balance I've ever seen in a human being."

"Well," she said with a sheepish grin, "my brothers and I used to play circus a lot. I alternated between wanting to be the tattooed lady, a trapeze artist or one of those people who balance glasses of wine on their heads.''

He raised one brow. ''I think I'd like to see that. So you're telling me that I've essentially been wasting my time. You already knew how to do this.''

She shrugged. ''You had a game plan. You're the expert. Did you think I would mess with that?''

''What I think is that Lionel underestimated you. You're such a fast learner I think perhaps you should be training me.''

She held out the book with a grin. ''Thank you, Ethan. Care for a stroll around the study?'' And then she swept into a low curtsy, looking up at Ethan from her position near the floor, a bright, eager look in her eyes.

Lord, what had Lionel and he been thinking when they chose this woman? She was a beauty, full of life and magic, and as innocent a woman as he had ever met. If he set her a task, she mastered it in an afternoon. If he asked her to do something, she tried it no matter how difficult. She'd watched *My Fair Lady* twelve times trying to pick up tips. A woman like that might well be conceited and proud and a complete manslayer, but Maggie wasn't conceited, and she had eyes that were brown and soft and oh, so vulnerable. From things she'd said and things she'd refrained from saying, he was certain that some idiot of a man had hurt her. She'd told him several times this week that a woman did not necessarily need a man. *She* did not. There was no doubt a good reason for her conviction.

And yet, here he was, a man who'd never done any woman any real good at all, a man who didn't even know how to handle a woman who clearly needed a future. And he was on the cusp of leading her straight into a situation where she might easily be harmed again if everything didn't go as planned. Maybe he should end this now.

But as she kneeled before him, she pulled a fan out of her pocket and expertly flipped it open. She fluttered her eyelashes at him over the ribs of the black and gold fan.

He nearly choked. With surprise, but also with something else. Something about the sight of those long-lashed brown eyes gazing up at him. A heat so powerful it threatened to melt him swept through him, and he couldn't help reaching for her, raising her to her feet.

"Did I do that wrong?" she asked suddenly, and the tiny slip of doubt made him realize that vulnerable as she was, going back would be more risky than going forward. Maggie was proud and stubborn. Being told to stop now would make her feel like a failure. Going forward at least gave her a chance to win.

He smiled down at her and realized that in pulling her up, he'd brought her in closer to his body than he'd intended.

"Who's been teaching you about fans?" he asked, gently pushing a tendril of her hair behind her ear.

She smiled sweetly. "Walter really knows his stuff."

He did choke then. "Walter is teaching you how to flirt."

"There's a lot you don't know about your butler," she confided.

"Maybe there's a lot I shouldn't know."

"Maybe. He's teaching me a few French phrases, too."

"I hope they're decent," he said with a smile. "I've

traveled with Walter. The women of France adore him, but I suspect most of his French is pillow talk.''

"Then maybe I'd better not tell you what he taught me.''

"Tell me.''

She rose on her toes and whispered in his ear, her warm breath drifting over his skin. He was going to have to warn her about doing that to a man. Later. "Is that right?'' she asked.

"It depends on what you want to do in the bedroom,'' he said with a smile. "I didn't catch that last word.''

And she gasped. "I thought I was asking you for directions to the parlor.''

Ethan couldn't help himself then. He picked her up and swung her around in a circle. "Maybe Walter did, too. Maybe that's why all the ladies descend on him if he's asking them for directions to their bedrooms. But I'd like to suggest that you refrain from that for now, angel.''

"I most certainly will,'' she said, as he gently let her go and the world swirled around them. "What subjects are we going to cover this afternoon?''

"Ah,'' he said, "something wild and exciting. Place settings. Shrimp forks. The order of seating.''

"Sounds riveting.''

"Um, but there's more. Aperitifs. Wine.''

"That's important?'' She looked worried.

"Only if you're in the company of those who are drinking. You will be. Are you all right, Maggie?''

"Sure,'' she said brightly, but her smile looked a bit forced. Once again Ethan wondered if he wasn't throwing too much at her. She'd been separated from her friends for days with only the company of himself and Walter and Poe. That couldn't be good for a woman.

"After we're done for today, I think we might con-

The Silhouette Reader Service™ — Here's how it works:

Accepting your 2 free books and gift places you under no obligation to buy anything. You may keep the books and gift and return the shipping statement marked "cancel." If you do not cancel, about a month later we'll send you 6 additional books and bill you just $3.34 each in the U.S., or $3.80 each in Canada, plus 25¢ shipping & handling per book and applicable taxes if any.* That's the complete price and — compared to cover prices of $3.99 each in the U.S. and $4.50 each in Canada — it's quite a bargain! You may cancel at any time, but if you choose to continue, every month we'll send you 6 more books, which you may either purchase at the discount price or return to us and cancel your subscription.

*Terms and prices subject to change without notice. Sales tax applicable in N.Y. Canadian residents will be charged applicable provincial taxes and GST.

If offer card is missing write to: Silhouette Reader Service, 3010 Walden Ave., P.O. Box 1867, Buffalo NY 14240-1867

NO POSTAGE
NECESSARY
IF MAILED
IN THE
UNITED STATES

BUSINESS REPLY MAIL
FIRST-CLASS MAIL   PERMIT NO. 717-003   BUFFALO, NY

POSTAGE WILL BE PAID BY ADDRESSEE

SILHOUETTE READER SERVICE
3010 WALDEN AVE
PO BOX 1867
BUFFALO NY 14240-9952

sider a dry run. A bit of company. Just a small group of trusted friends and Lionel. Maybe a few women to make you feel more comfortable.''

She bit down on her lip. ''That's probably smart,'' but she didn't look more comfortable. ''I need to practice with women nearby. They notice things.''

And he wondered what kinds of things women had noticed about her in the past that had put that look in her eyes. Probably that she was prettier than they were. No doubt something he couldn't make her forget with a few compliments. He was going to have to insist that Dylan and Spencer choose their female guests with great care. No one was going to have a chance to make Maggie feel out of place.

Although he couldn't put off the day of reckoning forever.

''Will you…will you be bringing a female friend?'' she asked suddenly.

He looked down at her, startled.

''Why do you ask that?''

She raised one delicate shoulder and studied the buttons on his shirt. ''It's been weeks since you and Ariel were together. Walter tells me you're rarely without feminine companionship.''

''I have feminine companionship. You.''

She frowned. ''I don't count.''

''You look like a woman to me.''

''I'm a woman in training, and you and I have a business relationship. We don't—well, we don't do the things you did with Ariel.'' Her voice was soft, her fingers fidgeted with the buttons on her blouse.

He placed his hand over hers to stop her, and they stood there, his hand over hers, just an inch away from her breast. A breast he very much wanted to touch, Ethan realized. More than he'd ever wanted to touch Ariel. He wanted to know for sure what lay beneath those prim little, white linen blouses she'd been wearing. He wanted to teach her more than how to choose the right fork. He wanted his hands up her skirt, his lips over hers and wandering lower.

Her heart was pounding beneath their palms, and he couldn't stop himself. He swooped down to kiss her, his lips a mere breath above hers.

"You shouldn't have to give up women because of me," she said.

And he drew back. Was she offering herself because she felt it was her fault that he was temporarily deprived?

He placed his fingertips where his lips should have been, over the softness of her mouth.

"Shh," he whispered. "I'm not giving up anything."

"You're sure?" she asked.

"Maggie, I chose this course of action. I'm the one who should be worrying about what you're missing out on."

"Oh, well, in that case," she said, looking slightly more sunny. "I'm just missing out on three weeks of sweeping floors and getting classrooms ready for the new school year. No need to feel bad about that."

But somehow he did. When he looked out that night and saw her during her nightly romp with Poe, he knew that he had taken her from her element and dumped her in his own, and that even though she was mastering all of his lessons, she was lonely and a bit scared. He was pretty sure she wasn't a woman who was often scared.

The next morning he was doubly sure. He came outside and found her arguing with a man who had come to repair part of the fence that Poe had dug up. Walter had, as usual, handled the transaction, so Ethan wasn't sure just what Maggie was doing gesturing from the house to the fence and back again. But as he drew closer, her words became clear.

"That's a ridiculous amount you're charging for a task such as this one. It's a simple repair I could do in two hours."

"Well, you're not the one doing it, are you?" the man demanded, sneering at her.

She sneered right back. "I could do it faster than you if I had the time, and I just might find the time and save Mr. Bennington the expense if you don't cease trying to rob him."

"Look, lady, I'm just trying to make a living."

"Then do it honestly. Just because Ethan Bennington has money doesn't mean you should triple your rates. Would you charge an ordinary homeowner this much for this kind of repair?"

"An ordinary homeowner couldn't pay me that much. Bennington can."

"Aha!" she said. "So you admit that you're cheating him."

"He's getting his fence repaired, isn't he?"

"Not by you," she said, crossing her arms. "You just take your tools and go on now. We don't need you here."

The man let fly a few choice words, and Ethan stepped forward, intending to place himself in front of Maggie, but she simply shot the man a contemptuous look. "And we won't hire anyone who speaks like that, either," she said, haughtily, and for a second Ethan was mesmerized by the look of supreme confidence and satisfaction on her face. She radiated authority, and when the man grumbled and picked up his tools and carted them off, she actually brushed her hands against each other and smiled. Sylvia Montcrief had nothing on his Maggie in terms of how high she could lift her chin. The lady deserved a round of applause and she was going to get one.

At the sound of clapping, she turned. "Uh-oh, you saw."

"And heard," he agreed.

"And now Walter has to find a new repairman."

"Who will probably charge me twice as much," Ethan teased.

For half a second she looked crestfallen. He was going to tell her that he didn't mean it, when she got a gleam in her eye.

"*You* will not repair the fence," he said. "No arguments."

She wrinkled her nose at him. "I wasn't going to offer. Well, okay, I was going to offer for a minute, there, but then I realized that I can't afford to get dirt beneath my nails and scratches on my arms. At least not in the next few weeks. *I* am temporarily a lady, you know," she said with a smile. "But I do know someone who can help. And Scott is very discreet."

Ethan frowned. "Scott?"

"An old boyfriend."

"One of the men who tried to grab you?"

She shrugged. "Maybe at first, but it didn't last. Scott decided he needed a different kind of woman. But we still see each other on business matters. He's a good handyman."

Ethan felt a dull roaring begin in his head. He didn't care if she had made her peace with Scott. At one time the man had hurt her. "Walter will find someone," he said.

"You don't trust me to recognize a good craftsman."

"I don't trust Scott."

"I told you he was discreet. He wouldn't talk about me."

"That's not the problem, Maggie. I don't hire people who don't have brains. And if the man didn't see what he had in you, he's not very smart. Walter will handle it," he said, and there was finality in his voice. Maggie opened her mouth to argue, but then she closed it again.

"All right," she said. "I guess I wouldn't want Walter thinking *I* didn't trust him to find the right person. I'll just give him a few pointers on what this type of job should cost. After all, he's helping me learn how to flirt, isn't he?"

And thank heavens for that was all Ethan could think, because there was no way he could survive a session of flirting with Maggie. She was much too kissable. He felt like a furnace whenever she was near. Maybe she was right about what abstinence was doing to him, but he'd be damned if he'd invite a woman to the dinner party and have Maggie be the only woman without a male partner. And he'd be more than damned before he'd invite a man to leer at her throughout dinner.

She was going to faint for the first time in her life. That was all there was to it, Maggie decided five days later. In just twenty minutes Walter was going to let five people who knew about the situation into the house, and they were all going to try and sit down and have a sophisticated dinner party. Only, the guest of honor wasn't going to make it because she was going to be passed out on the floor, brought low by such a tremendous bout of nerves that she couldn't eat, couldn't speak and she certainly couldn't move. She was going to let Ethan down.

Lord, she needed a stick of gum. Just one. For courage.

Just then a soft tapping sounded at her door. "Maggie, are you all right?"

She closed her eyes. Ethan. And he would look at her with those gorgeous silver eyes. She'd look up at those broad shoulders and that dark hair of his and that understanding look and feel like the biggest jerk of all time. Other women wouldn't fail him like this. Other women would know just what to do. If she were Ariel or someone like her, she wouldn't be apologizing for not being able to do something as simple as preside over a dinner. No, she'd be presiding over Ethan's bed and he'd be teaching her how to make love instead of how to walk and talk and eat and curtsy. As if Ethan would ever think of doing that with someone like her.

But the image of a shirtless Ethan in her bed had already been hatched.

"Come in," she said faintly.

In a black suit that showed off his broad shoulders, he was just as she'd envisioned him, only better. More tempting.

"Are they here already?" she managed to ask.

"Almost, but that's not what I'm here for."

That made her brain kick in. "I don't understand."

He smiled. "You know how I've been pushing you lately?"

"Oh, you haven't pushed," she began.

"I've pushed," he said forcefully. Okay, they had set a somewhat frenzied pace for their lessons. In the past few days they had concentrated on dance lessons, etiquette, titles of the rich and famous, how to handle a receiving line, how to lead a discussion so that no one felt left out, how to eliminate the flatness of her Midwestern accent and how to enter and leave a room.

The only thing they never had gotten to was that business about wine. She'd been so fascinated by the assortment of cutlery and the Bennington china that Ethan had let her play tea party and the wine had been forgotten. Tonight they would introduce that part of the curriculum, but she didn't want to think about that. Besides, Ethan was looking rather speculative.

"All right, you pushed a little," she agreed just to prompt him to continue.

"I pushed a lot," he said, insisting on making himself into an ogre. "And you, my lady, have been an angel of patience and a miracle of a student. For all your hard work and time and attention you've gotten nothing for yourself."

"I've gotten to live in this house."

"Which makes you feel a bit lost."

He noticed, she thought with a pang. "And you've given me a closet full of clothes."

"I notice you prefer your ripped jeans."

"Sorry," she said, wishing she'd been able to muster up a bit more enthusiasm for all the gorgeous dresses and tasteful slacks he'd bought her. "The new clothes are growing on me."

"I'm glad, but I want you to have one thing that you truly love. Besides Poe," he said, hitting on the one thing that truly did make her feel safe and secure. And he brought his hand from behind his back. He was holding a gold-wrapped box.

"A present?" she squeaked. "You brought me a present?"

He frowned. "You get them now and then, don't you?"

"Yes, sort of. At birthdays and Christmas. But I live with a lot of men who think that the brown bag the item came in is wrapping paper. Nothing like this."

And she took the box into her hands and held it as if it would break.

"You open it," she said. "I don't want to tear the ribbon."

"We'll do it together," he whispered, and he placed his large hands on hers and together they untied the length of gold ribbon that held the package closed.

When the silver box was revealed, Maggie removed the lid.

Her breath stopped. "These aren't for me."

"Only for you."

"Oh, but don't you remember how I—"

"They were made for you. You'll learn to walk in them, or maybe you won't and you'll simply wear them around your room or for one special man."

Maggie looked up into his eyes. She picked up the delicate silver heels that she'd tried on in Estelle's shop. They were so lovely, so fragile and lacy that she was almost afraid to hold them in her hands that were so used to wielding heavy tools. "I'm not the right kind of woman for these, Ethan," she said, trying to be very matter-of-fact though she wanted the shoes, she wanted to be the right kind of woman. "I'm not—I don't know—sexy enough."

She looked up straight into eyes that turned suddenly stormy. "Oh, you are so dead wrong on that, lady," and he took a step toward her.

Maggie's mind went nearly numb, but not numb enough not to notice that Ethan was looking at her as if he'd let down the gates of something powerful that lived within him. She should probably step back, say something sensible.

"I…" she began.

"*You,*" he said, advancing as he reached out and slid the flat of his hand against her waist, "are damned near the sexiest woman I've ever met in my entire life.'' His voice dipped low and his hand closed over her as he slowly, deliberately pulled her closer. ''You're like pure flame with all that wanton hair,'' he said, kissing her temple just beneath a curl that had slid forward. His lips felt like exquisite torture against her heated skin. She wanted them on her again.

''You have eyes that make a man think of watching them widen as he slides into you.'' He kissed his way lower. ''And your chin is strong and stubborn, a woman who won't let a man dominate her.'' He swooped low, and his lips just barely brushed her chin. ''And your lips,'' he added. ''Pure fantasy stuff. Open your mouth, Maggie.''

And as he took her lips beneath his own, she did just that. The fragile-as-cobwebs heels slid from her fingers as Ethan tunneled his fingers through her hair and taught her one more thing: how a kiss should feel. Like starlight in the middle of the day, like sun shining beneath the waves, hot and irresistible and so very unexpected and temporary that she knew she had to have it while she could.

She turned in his arms, slid her hands up his chest, leaned into him and kissed back as hard as she could.

It was good, so good but not nearly close enough, so she wriggled, trying to get closer. She wanted him all the way inside her, she wanted her lips fused to his.

His hand brushed her breast, and Roman candles went off behind her eyelids. She moaned into Ethan's mouth; she twisted, trying to get him to touch her there again.

But suddenly she was free, standing on her own, nearly falling. He reached out to steady her, then let go as soon as she was standing on her own. Somehow—she didn't know how, her mind was so muddled—he ended up on the other side of the room.

"*You* are temptation personified," he told her, "and I should have my face slapped for attacking you like that."

"But I liked it," she said. "You didn't? No, don't answer that."

He closed his eyes. She could see that his chest was heaving. "I didn't just like it," he said. "I craved it. To the point where I wasn't thinking straight. I was mad for you, even knowing that we have guests arriving in only minutes. I would have taken you right here on the floor, against the wall, however I could get you. You understand, Maggie?"

She understood that he wasn't happy about wanting her.

He shook his head as if to clear it. "I didn't come up here to seduce you." He held up his hand to stop her from saying she'd liked it again. "And I don't want to be one of those men you've known who grabbed without asking."

Maggie opened her mouth to say that he wasn't, that it hadn't been anything like her past experiences, but she was certain that saying that would only make things worse.

"I came up here to do something good for you," he said, his voice calmer now.

And he had, oh, he had, even though she was starting to feel her throat filling with tears. She would never know that feeling again, and it had lasted for such a short time. So what if it had been only momentary passion? It had been passion that she'd never felt, and it had been passion with a man she was beginning to feel far too much for, a man she didn't have anything in common with.

A man who was looking as if he'd like to beat him-self up very badly.

So she smiled, softly, gently. "Thank you for the shoes, Ethan. They're very beautiful. I'll wear them. I'll practice first, though. It's the nicest gift that any-one's ever given me."

His smile was sad, but at least he was smiling.

"Don't ever make the mistake of thinking you aren't woman enough, Maggie," he said gently. "You're all woman."

But she was the wrong woman for a man like him, and she'd known that from the start. This was not news, although it was a thought that caused a pain deep within her.

He couldn't know that. It wouldn't be good for him to know.

"Well, we have some people to impress. Let's go let them in and see what happens."

And with as much dignity as she could muster, given the fact that her lips were sensitive and swollen and her body was throbbing with need, Maggie slipped out the door and hoped that Ethan would follow.

Chapter Eight

The evening had started out well enough. Ethan couldn't have hoped for a better demonstration of just how well Maggie was progressing. Wearing a simple sea-green cocktail dress, she'd greeted their guests, directed the seating and kept a steady stream of light, polite conversation rolling.

Dylan and the woman he'd brought, April, and Spencer and his companion, Kate, had been pleasant company. Only Lionel had seemed less than relaxed, but that was to be expected. He had a great deal riding on this venture.

"You clean up pretty good, kid," he grumbled, and Maggie had given him a wink which had made him choke on his wine.

"To good company," Dylan had said, rising for a toast.

"And good friends," Spencer had seconded. Everyone had raised their glasses. Except Maggie.

Lionel frowned. "A toast has been made, you drink, girl."

A slight pink flush suffused her skin. "I don't really like wine."

"Don't like wine? You're to be attending a ball soon. People will be making toasts. Wouldn't be polite not to drink. You'll get noticed all right, but in the wrong way."

"Lionel," Ethan said stiffly. "Leave her alone."

Maggie shook her head. "No, he's right. I don't want people thinking the wrong thing. A toast to good company and good friends then," she said, taking a deep swallow of the wine.

Ethan could almost see a delicate shiver run through her. He leaned over and crowded her space. "You don't have to drink it, Maggie."

She smiled resolutely into his eyes. "This is the place to learn what I'm supposed to know. What kind of wine is this?"

"It's a Bordeaux. A 1970 Château Petrus."

"It's good," she said, rather dutifully, and Ethan smiled while Lionel sputtered. Château Petrus was an excellent and prestigious wine, and now that Maggie had taken a taste or two, she appeared to like it. She took a big swallow.

He leaned closer. "Sip it slowly, sweet stuff, or I'll be pouring *you* into your bed tonight."

"It's wine, girl, not soda pop," Lionel admonished.

Ethan was glad to see that his friends and their companions looked annoyed with Lionel. Everyone here knew about Maggie and that she was still learning.

"People can be so stuffy about their wine, eh, Dylan?" Spencer asked. "They never want you to get a good mouthful."

"I agree with Maggie. It's very good," and Kate Ryerson tipped her own glass up, even though Ethan could tell that she knew better. She was just trying to make his Maggie feel less self-conscious. He tipped his glass to her. That one was probably giving Spencer a bundle of trouble.

Dylan's April smiled sweetly at Maggie. "Men worry about the strangest things," she agreed.

And Ethan was surprised to see that never-get-involved Dylan looked delightfully disconcerted by his new companion's shy but frank manner.

"Wine is nothing to scoff at," Lionel muttered. "The girl is going to the top. She's got to know this stuff. Drink it like this." He demonstrated how to appreciate the flavor.

Maggie glanced questioningly at Ethan, and he felt warmth grow within him. She'd been taking instructions from him for two weeks now, and she allowed him to lead. It was good to know, however, that she wouldn't let herself be bullied.

"Only if you want to," he said gently. "You need to know a little, but you don't need to drink a lot."

She gazed up at him solemnly with those big brown eyes, and nodded. She took him at his word, too. Although she listened as he explained the background of the wine that arrived with each course, she drank only a few sips of each.

So when Ethan turned to her at dessert to ask her a question, he was surprised to find her smiling dreamily up at him, an obvious alcohol-induced amorous look in her eyes.

"You're so pretty," she said suddenly, softly, her voice just slightly slurred. "Isn't he pretty, Lionel? I love looking at him. Don't you?"

Ethan couldn't tear his gaze from her until he heard a slight coughing sound. He looked up to find Spencer and Dylan clearing their throats in an obvious bid to get his attention.

"Well, we surely should be going, shouldn't we, Spence? Big day ahead," Dylan announced.

"Oh yes, big day," Spencer agreed. "Are you ready, Kate?"

Kate was smiling a bit too widely. "Yes, of course," she answered. "Do not yell at her," she told Lionel. "You were the one who pushed her. April and I will call you," she said to Maggie as the four of them said their goodbyes and turned to go.

"Yes, and if you need a good remedy for a...a headache," April offered, "I have just the thing."

Lionel was holding his head in his hands. "She can't even hold her liquor."

Ethan felt a spurt of anger rip through him. "She doesn't have to. She's a fast learner. I'll wager that she'll remember everything we told her tonight, if her head is clear enough. Won't you, Maggie?"

She nodded vacantly, and Ethan knew she wouldn't remember a thing, but he also knew that she would feel guilty and make up for lost time by reviewing it all right away.

"Don't fuss at her, Lionel. This is my territory, not yours. We have a deal. Teaching Maggie is my right, and I'll do it my way. I won't have you badgering her. Come on, Maggie. Let's get you to your room, shall we?"

Gently he lifted her out of her chair. Then he threw caution to the wind and slipped his arm beneath her knees, lifting her up. She probably could have walked, but he didn't want her to have to remember the indignity of trying to steer her way across the room while under the influence.

"She can't hold her wine. She can't even hold her wine," Lionel moaned, and Ethan stopped him with a fierce look.

"I'm beginning to think that you can't either, Lionel, the way you're fussing. I'm sorry that I can't stay here and hold your hand, but there's no reason for you to stay. The party's over, such as it was. I'll ring Walter to see you out."

"You get her back to normal by tomorrow," Lionel ordered.

"Leave Maggie to me," Ethan said again. "She's—" He almost said "mine," but then he stopped himself. He didn't claim women for his own, and he didn't want to start now. "She'll be fine. I'll take care of her," he finished, then turned and strode off, holding Maggie close. He stopped to ring for Walter and then carried Maggie to her room.

The room was dark, and with Maggie in his arms, Ethan couldn't turn on the light. With only the pale lamplight shining in through the door, he gently let her down to stand, keeping her upright with one arm as he pulled the covers back.

"Time for bed," he whispered, and he helped her to sit down, then knelt at her feet and slipped her shoes off.

When Ethan looked up from his task she was gazing at him with that look of wonder in her eyes again. "Thank you," she said, and he wondered if she even knew what she was saying.

"Come on, sweet stuff, you need your rest." She would rest better without her dress on, but there was no way he was considering that, not with the way he'd lost control with her only this afternoon, and especially not when she was so vulnerable. It was only cloth and thread, and if the wrinkles proved permanent, he'd darn well buy her another. If he ever did see Maggie undressed, and he hoped he could keep himself from let-

ting that happen, he wanted her to be fully cognizant
of what was happening.

"Would you kiss me again?" she asked suddenly,
raising her lips to give him access. "I liked kissing
you. You're so good at it. You could give lessons,"
she said, trying to get up. "Yes, that's it, you give me
lessons in other stuff, and you really know your way
around…around lips. You could teach me. Kiss me,
Ethan?"

She somehow managed to rise to her knees and wrap
her arms around him. When he gazed into her eyes,
she looked so sweet and sincere and utterly, utterly
willing with those full pink lips, that he went weak-
kneed and hot.

"Maggie, don't do this. I'm not that strong, and you
don't know what you're saying."

"I know I want you to show me things. Man and
woman things. No one's ever shown me that."

Ethan closed his eyes. He felt like beating his head
against the wall. He felt like tumbling down onto the
bed with Maggie and sweeping her into his arms,
against his body. He wanted very badly to teach her
what she wanted to know.

But she was not herself, and he'd be damned if he
would take advantage of her innocence and her artifi-
cial lack of inhibitions. Besides, touching Maggie, even
if she were aware of what she was doing, just wouldn't
be right. She was a woman who needed things to be
solid and secure, and he would never be a solid and
secure kind of man.

And he liked it that way, he reminded himself.

"Ethan, please," she begged. "Touch me again."

And he cursed himself for ever having touched her
at all.

"You don't need me, sweet stuff," he said. "You

need some sleep. Now, in you go,'' he coaxed, slowly easing her back until she was lying down, then quickly pulling the covers around her before he could lose his mind and his strength of purpose. "Sleep tight,'' he whispered, but no matter his determination, he just couldn't resist dropping a kiss on soft curls that framed her forehead.

"Would you do this forever?'' she asked, her voice drowsy and confused.

"Do what?''

"I want you to—it's…it's so…Ethan—''

But he guessed he would never know what Maggie was going to say, because her words died away and she fell back on the pillows as sleep overtook her.

Ethan silently let himself out the door, pausing to look at her sleeping form just once before he let himself out.

She'd wanted him to teach her how to kiss. To teach her passion.

He took a deep breath and swore to himself.

There were many things he planned to teach Maggie, but someone else would have to teach her those lessons. In a few weeks he would move on as always, and nothing could induce him to be the next man to injure Maggie's soul.

Maggie woke the next morning with a headache. She wandered downstairs and found Walter waiting with aspirin and some sort of foul liquid, which he said would help.

"Looks and smells like it might kill me first,'' she mused, wincing at the sound of her own voice.

"Well, you won't know if you don't try.''

She tried. She was right about the taste, but Walter was right about the tonic's properties. After she'd sat there with her head in her hands for a while, the pain began to ease.

"Where's…where's Ethan?" she asked, although she was half afraid to meet him this morning. She had a vague recollection that she had said some stupid things last night. She just couldn't remember what they were. For some reason she had this horrid feeling that she'd asked Ethan to do something that had involved touching, and he'd turned her down. She wondered if she'd done something to drive him away.

But at that moment he came through the door smiling as if nothing had happened.

Relief flooded her. "Good morning," she said a bit too brightly, forcing herself to smile and pretend that there weren't still a few small men applying pickaxes to her temples.

"Don't worry about it," he said, as if he knew what she had been thinking. "We've all been there, bright eyes. It happens to all of us, doesn't it, Walter?"

"Oh yes. Ethan, here, once passed out right in front of the main entrance when he was still learning the ways of liquor. And I tipped a few now and then when I was a boy. You just got blindsided because you didn't have any practice. Now you know." And he smiled kindly as he left the room.

Well, she knew that she had gotten drunk.

"Was I…awful?" she ventured.

"You were your sweet, smiling self, Maggie, just a bit more exuberant," Ethan said. "How about taking the morning off?"

And make things worse by being undependable.

"I'm ready to move on to the next step, please," she managed to say, and she even managed to look Ethan in the eyes when she said it. "I'll only feel worse if I fall behind."

Was that concern she was seeing in Ethan's eyes? "All right, but it's your call. We'll stop whenever you need to."

"I won't need to," she promised, but she could swear Ethan was handling her with kid gloves today, abridging her lessons.

"More," she finally demanded. "You told me last week that I needed to know some of the history of Baltimore if that's where we're going to say I'm from. And I'm sure that was what you planned to tackle today. Let's have at it."

She purposely used that last phrase, hoping that by making him think she had more ground to cover than she actually did, he would forget her mistakes last night and concentrate on all they needed to accomplish.

Instead, he laughed. "Nice try, Maggie. I know Walter has been working with you on your speech patterns, and I know when I'm being manipulated. All right, we'll do it your way."

And suddenly she felt as if things were back to normal. She just had to know one thing.

"Ethan?"

He looked up.

"Be truthful with me. How drunk was I?"

He studied her for long seconds. "All right, you deserve the truth. Let's just say that I don't think you should drink wine at the ball. Especially not when you're in the company of eager young men."

She closed her eyes. "Oh no. I didn't, did I? I asked you to make love to me, didn't I?"

When he didn't answer right away, she knew the truth, but she needed to be looking at him when he told her. She forced herself to open her eyes and stare into his eyes.

"You asked me to kiss you. You asked me to touch

you," he said, his voice deep and thick. "That doesn't constitute asking me to make love to you."

She swallowed hard. "Well...okay. Well, then. Did you? Touch me, I mean?"

The hot, fierce look that swept his face made her feel weaker than she ever remembered feeling. Her knees threatened to buckle, and she braced herself against the table.

"I kissed your forehead and put you to sleep. You were fully dressed when you woke up. It would have been wrong to touch you when you didn't know what you were asking. Only a complete skunk would have done that."

"You could never be a skunk, Ethan."

His eyes turned dark and dangerous as she felt disappointment war with relief. Ethan hadn't touched her, and that should have made her glad, but there was a part of her that would have liked to have been woman enough to have broken through his defenses and that rigid self-control of his. On the other hand, any woman who had the opportunity to be in Ethan's arms and had no memory of the event, well, she supposed it was a good thing that Ethan was a gentleman.

Only, that wasn't quite a gentlemanly look in his eyes right now, and he was advancing perilously close. He braced his palms on the table as he stopped in front of her, then leaned close so they were nearly lip to lip.

"Since we're on the subject, no drinking at the ball," he whispered tightly. "No man in his right mind would turn down what you offered me if he didn't realize that you weren't quite yourself. I don't want any man making that mistake, and don't want you paying the price. I've asked enough of you as it is."

He was so close, the force of his words and their meaning so overwhelming that she could barely breathe. Maggie realized she was perilously close to making her request again, stone-cold sober this time. And then she would be a fool.

"It wouldn't happen," she managed to whisper.

"Promise me," he said. "Not one sip."

She opened her eyes wide, and he held both hands up and backed up. "I'm sorry, that was uncalled for. I don't have the right to give you orders."

But he wanted to. She wondered just how much she had begged him the night before. The thought made her queasy. To look pathetic and needy in Ethan's eyes...

"I promise," she said on a breath. "I've never really been a drinker, anyway. I suspect that my father knew something of my birth father. I think the man might have been an alcoholic, the way my dad felt so strongly about any of us having more than one or two beers."

"Is your birth father alive?"

She shrugged. "I don't think anyone knows that. I just think there might have been a problem."

But there wouldn't be a problem with her, not now that she had more than her father's disapproving looks to think of—she also had the concern in Ethan's eyes.

And so they went back to their studies, and the mood was easier...until Ethan heard the sound of cars coming up the driveway.

"A convoy," he surmised as they rose and looked out the window. "Oh, hell," he added.

He and Maggie turned to face each other in unison. She recognized the face from the pictures.

"Oh no," she moaned.

"Oh yes, sweet stuff. Afraid so. It's Sylvia Montcrief, the dragon socialite come to call."

"And that's not all," she said. "That car behind hers. The 1989 bomber. That's my father, the plumber, and he's not a man to tiptoe around the issue. When they meet up, the truth is going to come to light."

and have a great time. That's what Christmas is all about, isn't it? I'm sure my father won't mind one bit, and it will do everyone good to relax and enjoy a cup of punch together.

Chapter Nine

But Ethan was already moving. "I'll see to Sylvia. Have Walter meet your father and escort him to the side door."

She nodded, prepared to bolt off and find Walter.

"Oh, and Maggie?"

She skidded to a stop.

"Tell your father I'll be around to meet him in a minute. And tell Walter the red parlor."

She opened her mouth to protest. That was the best parlor.

But Ethan stopped her with one of those "take no prisoners" looks of his. "He's your father, Maggie. He rates."

A fine mist nearly blocked Maggie's vision. Her father was a good man, a hardworking, gruff, loving man, but as a blue-collar worker laboring in a very white-collar part of town, he had often not "rated" with those he worked for. That was part of the job, she supposed, and it had never seemed to bother him. But to have

MYRNA MACKENZIE   121

Ethan taking pains to make sure her father kept his
dignity, well, not every man would have considered it
necessary.

But there was no time for that, now. She sent Walter
to intercept her father, while Ethan stepped out to meet
Sylvia. Pacing across the carpet of the red parlor, Maggie could hear Ethan as he led Sylvia into the house.

"You're looking very well today, Sylvia. Let's just
go into the study and I'll get you something to drink
and you can tell me what I can do for you."

"The study? But the parlor is so much nicer—"

"Oh, Walter's in there today puttering around. Who
knows what he's up to? The man is always cleaning
things."

"And you let him have entirely too free a hand in
your household. If this house were mine—"

"Walter is like family, Sylvia," Ethan said gently
but firmly. And then he must have led her off toward
the study because her voice faded away and a door
clicked in the distance.

Maggie turned to see Walter ushering her father in.

"Dad," she said with genuine enthusiasm. He was
a strong man, but he looked lost in the midst of all this
opulence.

"Maggie, my girl," he said gruffly. "What in hell
are you doing here? I had the devil of a time finding
you. Contacted those auction people. I don't like this
setup. You're all dressed up and your hair looks different. Neater. Something's not right." But he took the
cigar that Walter was offering him. "Thank you,
Mr.—"

"Putnam," Walter supplied. "But just call me Walter."

"He the guy you're working for?" her father asked
Maggie.

"No, Ethan is—busy at the moment, but he'll be along as soon as he can."

"Probably talking to that dried-up old woman I saw coming in. Looked mean. I don't envy him. Not that I approve of him, either, you know. I checked him out. I hear things."

He looked around as if he didn't know what to do with the cigar. Walter pointed him toward a high-backed burgundy leather chair, lit his cigar and gave him an ashtray.

"Ethan's a fine man," Maggie said gently.

"I don't like you working here. You're a Todd, girl. What are you doing living up here with some rich, unmarried man who's probably used to having his way with a lot of women? And don't tell me you're not doing anything wrong. You haven't been home in two weeks. I know. I've called."

"Dad, I'm an adult, and I'm here to do a job. Ethan is my employer, not my lover. I explained that I was working."

Walter brought in a tray of coffee, tea and cakes. Maggie wondered what Ethan and Sylvia were talking about.

"It's summer. You should be out looking for a husband instead of holing up here with some rich womanizer who lives in a part of town people like us don't belong in."

Maggie crossed her arms and prepared to tell her father what she'd told him before. She was not going to shop for a husband and she was not going to go home until her job was done.

But at that moment she heard the sound of voices as if Sylvia was already leaving.

"I was sure I'd heard you had a new woman here.

I just wanted to welcome her to the neighborhood,'' Sylvia was saying.

"I've had a few people in doing jobs lately," Ethan explained. "Maybe that was what Ariel was talking about."

"More likely she was spreading rumors. You know how she is."

"Well, you know how rumors get started," Ethan said, and Maggie thought she heard laughter in his voice. "Thank you for stopping by, Sylvia. It was good of you to be so…neighborly."

The voices faded away. The distant sound of the door opening and closing reached Maggie's ears.

And then Ethan was standing in the doorway of the parlor, moving forward, holding his hand out to Maggie's father.

"Mr. Todd, it's a pleasure to meet you at last. Maggie's told me about you and your sons."

"I hope she told you that they all have muscles and know how to use them. Maggie shouldn't be here alone with you."

"Dad!"

Ethan shook his head. "Your father is worried, but you needn't be, Mr. Todd. Maggie is only here for the short-term. I'll have her back home in less than a week. Besides, Mr. Todd, I'm sure that you know that Maggie has her tools with her, and she definitely knows how to use them. Any man who would be so unmanly as to try to take advantage of her just might end up with a hammer blow to the head, don't you think?"

Matthew Todd's dark scowl turned slightly confused. "Well, Maggie always was one to stand up for herself."

"And it would be rather insulting to insinuate that she doesn't know her mind or that she doesn't have a good head on her shoulders, wouldn't it? I for one wouldn't think of even having such a thought. She's clearly a capable woman.''

"Maybe, but even capable women lose their heads now and then. I don't like this. I don't like it one bit. She could have gotten a good job, a normal job, one where she didn't have to live with an unmarried man. I'm thinking that I should just hang around here and see which way the wind blows.''

"You could do that,'' Ethan agreed, and Maggie nearly exploded. "But that might make Maggie feel as if you didn't trust her. What if I promised you that I wouldn't harm Maggie in any way? I wouldn't try to get her into my bed.''

"Why should I believe that?''

"Because I'm giving you my word.'' Ethan's voice spoke volumes. He'd been brought up by a man who ultimately couldn't be trusted, and it meant everything to him to prove that he was not such a man. Her father wouldn't know that story, but he could hear it in Ethan's voice and see it in his eyes.

"My word of honor,'' Ethan said again in a stern but quiet voice. His eyes were dark silver and forceful, his jaw tense.

Matthew Todd had the good grace to look slightly ashamed.

"Well, I suppose that would do it. That and the fact that you're right. Maggie does have a good head on her shoulders. She knows where her place is.''

He stayed just long enough to exchange a few catch-up stories with Maggie, but soon he was taking his leave. Shaking Ethan's hand. Shaking Walter's hand.

"Take good care of her,'' he warned.

"She's golden,'' Ethan said. "I promise.''

This should make things so much easier, Maggie

thought as he left. There wasn't even the tiniest chance that Ethan would make love with her now. She supposed she should be happy.

Instead she felt a sense of loss. Silly when there hadn't ever been any possibility of anything happening between her and Ethan, anyway.

She needed to keep reminding herself of that, and suddenly Maggie felt hot and restless and uncomfortable. Her father was right. She did not belong here and she never would.

The words seemed to echo through her head. She needed action, good hard work.

"Excuse me, I have to...to do something," she said, hoping that Ethan couldn't read her thoughts.

"Maggie, I'm sorry," he said.

"He's right, you know. I'm all wrong for this place."

"Maybe it's just that this place is all wrong for you."

She tried to smile. "Thanks for saying that, but I've been here before. When Scott left me for Leslie, it was because he'd realized that he didn't want a woman who felt more at home with her head under the sink fixing the pipes instead of over the sink washing the dishes. He didn't want a woman who felt more at home in work boots than in satin slippers. I didn't belong with Scott any more than I belong here."

He shook his head, crossing the room in three strides.

"Who died and made Scott an expert on women? Sounds to me like the man was missing something vital."

"What?"

"His senses, his eyes, you and all that you are." He took her face in his hands and brought his lips to hers.

Gently he brushed his mouth back and forth over hers. She parted her lips and he came inside, the flavor of Ethan spinning through her, consuming her, heating her instantly and filling her with want.

She reached for him, pressing herself close, her breasts flattening against his chest, her thighs against his so that she could feel him growing hard against her.

"Ethan?" she whispered, and he groaned and pulled away.

"You make me want to do crazy things," he said. "To break my word when I just promised I'd leave you untouched."

"I trust you," she protested.

"Don't." The single word was harsh, and when she looked into his eyes she saw naked desire. "It would be a mistake for both of us if we got involved. I'd hurt you, Maggie. My father was an unfeeling man who cared nothing for the fact that he had a wife and son. I was no sooner born than he was off chasing the next woman. He taught me the value of remaining uninvolved, but I still made some of his mistakes. I was engaged to a woman who knew our marriage was to be based on business and mutual companionship, but I still managed to hurt her badly. Love causes pain and dependence, and I could never pursue that. Damaging Vanessa was ugly. I don't ever want to harm a woman again. And you're much too warm and giving for a man like me. Your father was right. I gave my word, and I'll do my utmost to keep that word. But I am human, and I want you in my bed, so don't trust me. Given the right circumstances, I'd take you and let all my promises be damned."

She stared up at him solemnly, seeing the raging emotions battling in his eyes. A child ignored, watching his mother betrayed and his father proven to have feet of clay. Standing by as he learned he was capable of hurting another, possibly of hurting *her* given the right circumstances. But he wanted her, and she—oh yes, she wanted him. She wondered if she was capable of sharing a night with him and surviving the aftermath.

"What kind of circumstances?"

"Maggie," he warned.

"Under what circumstances would you—would you make love to me? I'm not asking for commitment, Ethan. You know that I don't want a man forever any more than you want a woman."

And she stepped up against him. She felt his heart pounding, felt the rugged male length of him, breathed in the scent that was all Ethan. She lifted her lips to his.

He stared down at her, naked longing written in his eyes.

He leaned, he took her lips.

His kiss was sweet, so very sweet, and she wanted it sweeter still. She wrapped her arms around him, felt herself being lifted off the ground as he pulled her tight against him.

"Maggie," he breathed against her lips, and there were worlds of want in his voice. There was deep regret at what he was about to do.

She was going to damage him badly if she forced him over the edge. His word was all. Hadn't she just thought that very thing moments ago?

If he gave his word and then broke it, if she pressed him beyond the point of no return, pressed her body against his until he forgot who she was and who and what *he* was, forgot everything except the need of a man for a woman, any woman, then he might break. Any man might break, but in Ethan the wound would go deep. Any pleasure there might be would be forever marred.

"Maggie, Maggie," he whispered her name as he kissed her lips, her eyelids, her chin, and bent his head to press his lips against her neck as she arched to give him access.

For two seconds, three, four, she reveled in what she was doing, what she was feeling, wanting, finally having, and then, as tears gathered in her eyes, she placed her hands on his arms. She pushed.

Immediately he released her.

Her lips trembled.

He swore. His eyes were dark and angry. "Damn it, Maggie, I—did I hurt you? I'm sorry for losing my head."

She shook her head violently, fighting the tears. "I pushed you. You told me. I didn't believe you."

"Doesn't matter. I'm not an animal. I have some sense of self-control. Usually."

He looked completely put out with himself, and she just had to smile and try to stop him from beating up on himself. She was the one. She had wanted him to want her so badly, she had wanted *him* so badly that...

"Hey, it's been a stressful day. Who has any self-control left?" she teased. "Not me. What woman in her right mind wouldn't try to drag the great Ethan Bennington into her bed if there was the least little chance that it could happen? You know me, the opportunist. Not a shred of decency or any sense of right and wrong."

He stared at her, then shook his own head. "You, Maggie Todd, are a liar."

"Well, I did want you to make love to me," she confessed. "You *are* incredibly sexy, Ethan, and it would have made a great addition to my scrapbook. I could have pasted the memory right next to my award for best custodian of the year.''

''If you'd wanted me, Maggie, you know damn well you had me. I wouldn't have stopped.''

''Oh yes, you would have.''

His look said that she was a liar again.

''I barely tried to wriggle and you let me go. If I'd said no, you would have done your best to let me have my way.''

''Would you have said no if it had gone any further?''

''I hope so,'' she said honestly. But she wasn't sure if she would have been able to stop if she'd waited any longer. Good thing she'd ended it in time. Lots of room for heartache if she ever really did climb into Ethan's bed.

Lots of room for pleasure, too. That little thought tried to sneak in, but she blocked it off.

''I think I need to go fix something,'' she said suddenly.

''Maggie, you've checked every electrical outlet, tightened every screw, patched the plaster and oiled the squeaky doors. What could be left?''

''There's always something that needs maintaining,'' Maggie said, as she left to change her clothes. She wasn't kidding. She really needed to find a project for this afternoon. It was a good reminder of the world she really was meant for, and it kept her from fidgeting and thinking of getting Ethan naked.

But as she passed by the front door a few minutes later, the bell rang, and she looked out the peephole, then pulled it open. No point in dragging Walter out when she was right here.

''Lionel!'' she said with more enthusiasm than usual.

The old man's brows rose in surprise, but the greater surprise was the smile he returned.

"You're getting used to it here, aren't you?" he asked. "Fitting in?"

Oh, how could she break his heart by telling him she'd just realized that she would never fit in?

"You came to talk to Ethan?"

He nodded. "The man hasn't called me in three days. He knows I want a progress report. Maybe you'd like to fill me in on what's been going on."

She wrinkled her nose and grinned at him. "I don't think it would be right to issue my own grades. I'll let Ethan help you. I was just going to get my tools."

He frowned. "I thought you'd stopped that."

"Lionel, let's get one thing straight. I am a woman who fixes things. You have anything that needs fixing? Any fences that need mending? Any pipes that need patching or bathrooms that need to be recaulked? If you do, then I'm your woman. For you, I'll even do it for free, because you're such a grumpy old sweetie." And she smiled and quickly kissed him on the cheek.

He gasped, he nearly wheezed, she was sure he trembled slightly. "No, no repair jobs," he said, and his voice was twice as gruff as usual. "Shouldn't you be wearing a dress?" he grumbled, looking at her jeans.

"Ethan lets me wear what I want when my lessons are over."

"Ethan is a fool, and I'll tell him so when I see him."

"Um, Lionel?"

"What?" he barked.

"Ethan's standing right behind you, and he's been there for the past few seconds. I think you already told him."

"Well, then he knows. You're a fool, Ethan. This woman needs discipline."

"Ah, Lionel, I know, but she has a silver tongue. She says please, and I just turn to butter inside. What's a man to do?"

Maggie was pleased to see that the old teasing look was back in Ethan's eyes. He grinned as Lionel sputtered.

"You're not supposed to be letting her lead you around, man. You're supposed to be making a lady of her. How do you expect to do that if you can't even tell her no when she asks to wear those raggedy pants?"

"Well, she does look rather nice in them, doesn't she?"

"That's beside the point."

"And what is the point again? I forget sometimes when Maggie charms me so."

By now Lionel was starting to smile a bit, too. "Enough with your teasing, Ethan. Are you going to give me a rundown of her week? Is she doing well?"

"She's a veritable wonder, Lionel. A wonder of a woman."

And on that note Maggie left them. Ethan's voice had sounded low and intimate when he'd made that last statement. She was still too needy to trust herself not to start mooning after him when he used that soft, sexy tone.

Besides, she was beginning to suspect that Ethan had a soft spot for cranky old Lionel. She was beginning to have a soft spot for him herself, but she thought he might need a man to talk to now and then.

And Ethan, as she knew all too well, was very much a man.

She was a woman with an itch for a man she

couldn't have, in a world where she would never fit, no matter how many lessons Ethan gave her. The fact was that she preferred denim to satin, she preferred bare feet to shoes, and she didn't know how to be near Ethan without wanting to tackle him.

She sorely needed a taste of home. Where were her tools? If she didn't fix something soon, she would go crazy—or else she would attack Ethan and force him to make love to her.

Chapter Ten

Maggie had been like a caged creature who needed to run for the rest of the day, Ethan thought as night began to settle. Estelle had told him that she'd fidgeted and worried so much that a pin had gouged her when Estelle had come to give her the last fitting for her ball gown. She'd worried aloud about tripping over the hem at the dance, about spilling something on her dress, about a hundred other things.

The image of her lost in his arms earlier in the day stalked him, and he felt an ache so deep he didn't dare examine it. She was like electricity, amazing, untamable, alive. Furthermore, she'd been a good trouper and a quick learner, but this situation with both of them fighting desire, and this house where she didn't feel comfortable, was taking its toll on her.

He wanted to free her.

He wanted to ask her to never leave him, but knew that feeling would pass.

Right now he was simply concerned about the circles

under her eyes. After the fitting she'd gone off for dancing lessons, and after dinner she'd been so antsy that she had asked him, no, begged him, if he and Walter wouldn't like to play a board game. Of course, he didn't have any board games, but she'd looked so eager. Apparently, she and her brothers and even her father often relaxed in the evenings this way, so Ethan declined to tell her he didn't even possess a single game.

Instead, he and Walter made a few quick phone calls to some local stores, and within hours all three of them were seated at one end of the huge dining room table.

"Don't you dare let me win," Maggie warned Ethan as she rolled the dice and moved her piece.

"I'm going to destroy you," he told her, raising one brow.

"Oh, really? Well then, what do you think of this?" she asked, forcing him to move his piece back to his home base.

"I like it just fine," Ethan replied, slipping in a move that forced her to move her piece halfway back around the board.

She blinked, then laughed. "That *was* pretty ruthless," and Ethan could tell she loved the fact that he refused to make things easy for her, even though she knew the rules better than he did.

But her next move left him limping. "You really are a merciless woman," he commented dryly, but he grinned when he said it. She was a delight to watch, and to see her happy and smiling and at ease after the dipping and rocketing emotions of the day filled him with relief.

In the end Walter quietly stole beneath both their defenses and trounced them soundly. And that was fine, too.

But now Maggie appeared worn-out and tired.

"Go to bed, bright eyes," he told her gently, indulging himself by tucking one silky curl back behind her ear. When his fingertip brushed her earlobe, she shivered slightly and Ethan placed his hands behind his back. No more touching for today.

She shook her head. "Poe's expecting me for his nightly romp."

And the time with the dog was good for her, but she didn't have any energy left.

"I'll take him out."

Her eyes widened.

"He *does* know me," he reasoned. Of course, he never took the dog out, but he'd watched the mutt worm his way into her heart and give her pleasure. How could a man help feeling a fondness for an animal that could do that?

Maggie nodded solemnly. "Just remember, he likes to have his ears scratched, and Walter will show you where his toys are. Don't forget to let him back inside when your walk is over. He might dig under the fence again, and we'd have to find another repairman. And—"

Ethan gently raked his fingertips across her lips, silencing her. "I'll learn," he told her. "In time."

"I'm sure you're a very fast learner."

Later, when Ethan found himself out on the lawn with the big black dog frisking nervously beside him, he glanced up at the window to find Maggie peeking out.

"Looks like we'll have to show her we're all right, won't we, my friend?" he asked the dog, who tilted his head curiously.

Ethan held out the dog biscuit that Walter had given him, and Poe took it from his hand with an almost delicate precision. He settled on the ground and devoured his treat, licking his paws. Then he looked up at Ethan.

"Good?" Ethan asked.

Poe wagged his tail daintily.

"Ah, our lady has taught you manners, hasn't she? But she's also taught you to play, I think."

Ethan threw the red squeaky toy that was, he'd been told, the dog's favorite, the doll whose painted ears were well chewed. Poe gave a great gleeful bark and raced after the toy, and Ethan raced with him. The wind rushed through his hair, the grass soft beneath his feet. When Poe retrieved the toy, he turned to Ethan with an expression that could only be called pride or as close to it as a dog could get.

Ethan knelt, scratching Poe behind the ears.

"It's a lovely evening for a run, isn't it, my friend?"

Poe wagged his tail as if to agree.

What a great animal, Ethan thought, and he settled down cross-legged on the cool evening grass and made friends with the big dog that had answered the call in Maggie's sweet heart.

He glanced up at the darkened room. Maggie had surely gone to bed, but just for a second he thought he saw her with her chin resting on her arms, her arms resting on the window ledge. He'd bet she was kneeling on the floor in her bright frog pajamas with her pretty legs peeking out.

"Get some sleep, Maggie," he called softly. "He's fine."

"I know." Her small voice came back, faint but happy. "I will go to sleep. I need to start saving my energy. The big day's almost here, and I don't want to fall asleep in front of the cream of Chicago. Wouldn't want to mess up."

"Looks like we're just going to have to work harder to make sure that she doesn't overdo," he whispered to the dog.

And Poe looked up at him with soulful eyes and licked his hand, a clear assent if Ethan had ever seen one.

"So how do you think we can help Maggie?" he asked.

But for once the big dog had no answers.

It was the fourth of July, just two days away from the day of reckoning, or as Maggie liked to think of it, the day when the delicate crust of Chicago would meet the soggy bottom of Chicago. She was practicing her French, her dancing, her grammar, her small talk. Walter was coaching her, Lionel was coaching her, Ethan was coaching her, but now and then Walter had to see to the house, Lionel had to see to his restaurants and Ethan had to see to his firm.

"A good time to practice the most difficult stuff," she decided, pausing before the hallway mirror.

"Why, good evening, Mr. Llewellen," she said with what she hoped was a sweet smile. "Yes, it *is* a warm evening. Very warm." She waved a pretend fan and fluttered her eyelashes. She looked up at what had to be a very tall man. Well, he had looked tall in the picture Ethan had shown her. "Thank you, yes, I *would* like a glass of water, but then we wouldn't get to talk. Why don't I go with you, Raymond? Is it…all right if I call you Raymond? Will you mind if I take your arm?"

She pretended to place her arm on the invisible man in the mirror, elevating her own slightly. "You *are* tall, Raymond. They say that tall men command authority. My great-great-grandfather the duke was reputed to be tall, but I doubt he was as tall as you.'' She leaned closer as if to listen to something the man was saying. At that moment she saw a bit of movement in the mirror and whirled to find Ethan lounging in the doorway.

''You could have at least knocked,'' she told him.

''The door was open,'' he said, studying her with careful, dark eyes. ''Was that Raymond Llewellen you were flirting with?''

''I wasn't flirting.''

He raised one brow. ''The man would have been taking his shirt off to show you his muscles in another minute or two. And what would you have done then?''

She struggled for a deep breath. ''Laughed? Or maybe simply informed him that a ballroom was no place to start shedding his clothes.''

''Which would have led him to suggest that you go somewhere more intimate so that he could disrobe in privacy. With you.'' His eyes had turned stormy, his jaw was set in steel.

Maggie was very aware that the man she really wanted to be flirting with was standing before her, shooting daggers at her with his eyes. But he wouldn't want her to admit that.

''Walter tells me I need to know the gentle art of flirting. If I'm doing it wrong, then teach me.'' Her words were a whisper. She hoped that she didn't look or sound pathetic. To have Ethan thinking that of her so close to the date of the ball was too excruciatingly painful to consider.

''You don't need to flirt,'' he told her flatly. ''Just talk to the men the way you talk to Walter and to Lionel.'' She noticed he didn't mention the way she talked to him. No doubt he was remembering the day when she'd tried to seduce him. He was probably regretting ever having brought her into his life. It had been almost three weeks. This must be getting pretty old for him. He was reputed to be a man who moved from one woman to another on a regularly rotating schedule.

"But if a man should flirt with you," he said with those beautiful, soulful eyes, "you treat him the way you treat your brothers."

He looked so tense, so worried, that she couldn't help trying to tease him into feeling better. "You mean I should offer to arm wrestle him for my honor?" she asked.

And Ethan chuckled. "No arm wrestling," he said with mock sternness. "The bodice of that dress you'll be wearing just might not withstand any vigorous movement, and I don't want to have to quell a riot. Lionel would shoot himself, and I—"

She looked up at him expectantly.

"Well, it's not the best idea," he finished lamely. "If a man makes you uncomfortable, either treat him like an elderly uncle with a gentle word of dismissal or come get me and I'll make sure he understands that you are not his for the taking."

Maggie felt suddenly breathless. Ethan was staring at her as if he intended to take her right here. She stared up at him. She might even have swayed slightly, leaning in toward him.

He closed his eyes for half a second, then he leaned in close and dropped a light kiss on her forehead.

"We'll get through this, Maggie," he promised. "With no bruises. You're going to be the belle of the ball. Men will be taking numbers just to get near you. You're going to have the evening of your life. I intend for you to enjoy it. Anyway, that's the day after tomorrow. We still have some time."

Suddenly she smiled. "Yes, and it's the Fourth of

July today. I think I've done enough flirting for the day. It's time to get down to the really good stuff.''

For a moment Ethan looked shocked, and Maggie allowed herself to laugh.

''Not *that* good stuff.'' She rolled her eyes at him. ''Fourth of July good stuff. I've got everything planned. You just sit back and watch.''

Maggie jumped into the holiday the way she jumped into everything, Ethan mused a short hour later. Within a matter of minutes, she had a picnic planned and had herded him, Walter and Poe out onto the lawn where she set up a blanket, insisting that a picnic wasn't a true picnic if a table was involved.

''It's not fair to the ants,'' she said with a smile.

''Of course. We must be fair to the ants,'' he agreed. ''Any other type of insect life we need to concern ourselves with?''

''Not at a picnic. I love your yard, Mr. Bennington.''

''Don't tell my gardener that you called it a yard, will you? He's touchy about those kinds of things. I'll have you know that this is the west lawn.''

''Which means that it's ten times bigger than a yard, I suppose?''

He smiled. ''And ten times more pretentious.''

''But pretty.''

''Very pretty,'' he said, looking at her flushed cheeks and the way her eyes sparkled beneath that mass of auburn curls.

''Time for games now,'' she said, hopping up. ''Did you bring the horseshoes, Walter?''

''Yes, Maggie,'' Walter said. ''You'll show us how?''

''This is the part I love,'' she said, dropping her voice to a low, seductive whisper and batting her eyelashes at Ethan. "The part where I get to be the teacher."

She was a good teacher, too, Ethan thought, full of enthusiasm and patience. And afterward she rewarded them with a red-white-and-blue cake topped with sparklers. "I had Walter order it," she said. "Baking is not my specialty."

"Um, but if a man wanted to arm wrestle or pound a few nails…" Ethan mused.

She nodded. "I would be the woman he was looking for."

Her words hit Ethan with a soft impact. *The woman he was looking for.* He shook his head, tucked into the cake and shoved the words away.

"This is nice," Walter mused, leaning against a tree in an uncustomarily casual fashion. "Rather homey."

"This is small potatoes," Maggie said. "You should see the Fourth of July when my family gets started. Horseshoes *and* baseball *and* volleyball. Two grills going at full tilt, two cakes and cherry pie and lots of friends and music."

"Sounds nice," Ethan said, too full and relaxed to do anything but lean back and watch Maggie. But this is nice, too, he thought. This was something he'd never had, this easy camaraderie, this stopping just to do something simple and fun and cozy. This felt like family, and he'd never really had that. Never wanted it, at least not in many years.

"Come on," Maggie said, climbing to her feet. "You can't just sit after you've eaten. You'll fall asleep."

Then she giggled because Walter *had* fallen asleep. "We'll let him rest," she said softly, digging a second blanket out of the picnic basket and gently tucking it between Walter's head and the rough tree bark. "He helped me plan the food. He's earned this. But you," she said, "that's different. We don't want to wake Walter, so maybe we should talk somewhere else. I'll race you to the oak tree outside the rose gardens."

And she took off at a dead run, her slender body strong and supple and fast.

But Ethan was no softie. Startled by her challenge, he lost a few seconds, but only a few. Leaping to his feet, he dashed after her as her hair streamed about her, a bright contrast to her pale yellow blouse and white shorts.

She shrieked and laughed as he drew close, then covered her mouth, glancing back to see if she'd disturbed Walter. Poe, caught up in the excitement, danced around the lawn.

"Don't look back, Maggie, there's a man chasing you," Ethan teased.

"Ah, but he's a slow man," she said, her voice light and breathless.

"Maybe usually, but not when the woman he's chasing is a prize with long, lovely legs and a sassy mouth. That could drive a man to run faster, to catch her and see if he could claim those legs and silence that mouth with his own."

His words had an effect. Maggie glanced over her shoulder, her eyes wide with surprise.

Ethan realized that his teasing wasn't all teasing. Flushed and breathless as she was, her chest heaving, her pretty, muscular legs long and strong, she was a woman any man would love to catch into his arms.

But the moment she looked back, she made a mistake. The oak tree loomed, its roots catching her toe and tripping her.

Maggie tumbled, all long hair and arms and legs.

Ethan's only thought was to keep her from hitting

the ground as he dove beneath her in a classic baseball slide, reaching out and catching as much of her as he could, then rolling and tumbling among the roots and grass until they came to a breathless stop.

"I'm sorry," he crooned, when he could catch his breath. "I'm so sorry I distracted you, sweetheart. Are you all right? Are you cut? Scratched? Alive?" And he gently began to feel her limbs, raking his hands along her arms and down to her legs.

When he touched her thigh, she gasped, and he turned his face to hers and realized her mouth was half a breath from his. Her hair was tangled and tossed about her face. He gently touched her cheek with shaky hands and smoothed her hair back off her forehead. She still hadn't answered him. "Maggie?"

"I'm all right," she said, looking down at her body. "Just a rip in my blouse and a tiny scrape on my knee, but that's okay. No one at the ball will see a bandage beneath my gown."

But he didn't care whether someone would see it or not. He gently slid his fingers down to the area where she'd scraped herself, steering wide of the wound. "I shouldn't have teased you," he said, which made her smile and shake her head.

"Ethan, I get much worse than this all the time in my job. I do physical labor, and that means cuts and scrapes and bumps and bruises. This is absolutely nothing, but you—your poor back must be aching the way you landed. That was a masterful save, Mr. Bennington. The Cubs might like to have you on their team if you'd be willing to try out. Not bad for a rich boy, Ethan." And she smiled reassuringly into his eyes.

He couldn't help himself. Leaning toward her, he stared at those pretty pink, smiling lips. Angling his head, he moved closer as she closed her eyes and parted her lips.

"Ethan! Ethan, are you there?" And as if in slow motion, both he and Maggie turned toward the voice. At that moment an attractive, plump brunette woman rounded the bend and cast startled eyes on them. She'd been holding a purse, but she dropped it, a shocked, slack look on her face.

Mentally Ethan groaned, but he held his emotions in check. Gently he untangled his legs from Maggie's. He eased her body off his, then rose, holding out his hand to help her up.

"Hello, Vera," he said, looking back over his shoulder at the woman who had picked up her purse and was dusting it off.

"I...I tried the house, but there was no one there. There's always someone there, and your car was in the garage when I peeped inside," Vera stammered. "Aren't you going to introduce me to your friend, Ethan?"

Maggie had gone pale. She took the hand Vera was extending. "Hello." Maggie's voice was barely a whisper.

Ethan wasn't sure who was more shocked, Maggie or Vera. He was sure it looked bad from either angle. He and Maggie wrapped around each other on the grass. No question what Vera was thinking, or Maggie, either. Vera was definitely part of the "cream" Maggie was always talking about. She would be at the ball, and Maggie did not have the kind of face a person forgot in two days.

But Maggie, sweet, chatty Maggie seemed incapable of words.

"Vera," he said, taking charge. "I'd like you to meet my guest, the granddaughter of one of my grandfather's old business associates from Baltimore and the great-great-granddaughter of the Duke of Tarrington. She's only just arrived in town. I was going to show her the rose garden, but you know the way these old oaks are. Roots like boulders. They trip you up and you tumble like dominoes.''

Vera smiled nervously. She glanced down toward where Ethan and Maggie had been linked only seconds ago.

All right, his words *had* sounded lame. The expression on Vera's face told him she knew he had been on the verge of kissing Maggie. But the bit about Maggie being related to one of his grandfather's business associates sounded plausible, and that was really all that was important. If he had to, he would make sure people thought that he had seduced an innocent woman of good birth. It would produce sympathy for Maggie, and no one would have trouble believing it of him.

''The roses are so…pretty, don't you think?'' Maggie's voice came out suddenly, tense and soft and utterly naive. Ethan could almost feel her shaking.

''Would you like to join us?'' Ethan asked Vera. ''The Fourth of July is a perfect day for a stroll around the gardens.'' He stressed the name of the holiday, and Vera blushed lightly.

''Actually, it's the holiday that brought me here. Mother sent me to ask if you'd like to come to the fireworks display we're putting on. It's so much cozier than going all the way into the city. She said she'd meant to ask you and then forgotten about it.''

Well, at least her words sounded as lame as his, Ethan thought. Vera was clearly here to spy. He wondered just what rumors had been circulating these past three weeks between Ariel and Sylvia. Since he'd barely left the house, he wouldn't know.

"I'm afraid we won't be able to make it. Ms. Todd is very fatigued. All that traveling, you know. And she's to be the guest of honor at the party Lionel Griggs is giving in two days. Lionel knew her grandfather, too. Will you be there?"

Vera looked as if she'd just discovered gold or a good bit of gossip. "Of course I'll be there, silly," she said. "Everyone will be. I hope you're...recovered by then, Ms. Todd."

"Thank you. I'm sure I'll be feeling much better soon," Maggie said quietly.

Together they watched Vera hurry away across the grass as quickly as her Rubenesque body would allow. Her ankles twisted as she hit a few rough places, but it didn't seem to bother her. Clearly she was a woman who had gotten what she'd come for.

Vera's car was far down the driveway when Maggie collapsed to her knees. She covered her face with her hands. "I can't believe I was sprawled out like a wanton on the grass, that my hair and clothes were a mess, and worse, that I couldn't think of a single intelligent thing to say. Everything's ruined. We're dead in the water. Now you're not going to get to represent Lionel's restaurants. You won't be able to mend your grandfather's business. How could I have been such a ninny? Did I really ask if she thought roses were pretty? Of course she thinks so. Everyone in the world thinks so."

In spite of the fact that she was partly right about the sad state of things, Ethan couldn't help but smile at Maggie's tirade. "Hush, Maggie. It was an accident. I should have been more aware of what was going on. I knew this might happen."

"You did?"

He nodded and tried to ease the shock of what he

was going to say next. "I knew that Ariel, angry as she was when she left here, would have to spread her suspicions about my having a new woman and that she would tell Sylvia. Sylvia's a gossip, but she takes a special interest in any gossip that concerns me."

Maggie frowned and shook her head, a confused look in her eyes. "What does that have to do with Vera?"

Ethan let out a long sigh. "Everything. Vera is the reason Sylvia takes such an interest in my affairs. Sylvia once hoped that Vera would become the next mistress of Bennington Manor. Vera is Sylvia's daughter."

Maggie blinked. "The daughter of the dragon lady?"

"I'm afraid so."

"And she just found us on the verge of...you know."

"Well, I don't think we would have done it right here. Not with Walter snoring just across the lawn," he said soothingly.

"And I acted like a total idiot in front of the daughter of the woman who is going to either give us the thumbs-up or the thumbs-down? The woman who has the power to wield the guillotine?"

"I don't think they do anything that drastic anymore," Ethan assured her, trying to tease her out of her panic. "Besides, I thought you did very well."

"Poe could have performed better than I did."

"But he wouldn't look half so entrancing in a ball gown."

Maggie still didn't smile.

"Don't worry, Maggie," he said, catching her hand in his and brushing his thumb across her palm. "It's not over until it's over, you know."

But the truth was that it would be over very soon. And then he would either get what he wanted...or he wouldn't.

Chapter Eleven

Maggie had a strong urge to scream, but that wouldn't have done Ethan any good, and she really, really needed to do something good for Ethan.

It was becoming increasingly clear that she had made a serious mistake yesterday, and she wasn't just talking about the incident with Vera.

It had hit her when she'd been racing with Ethan, when he'd cushioned her fall, when he'd bent to kiss her. She was in love with Ethan.

The fact that she couldn't have him held no sway. She couldn't stop loving him, and given her situation she couldn't do the sensible thing, as she would have done had he been any other forbidden man: she couldn't leave to protect herself.

"Just two more days," she whispered to herself as she looked up from the book she was studying. It was a relief to know that she would soon be released from the exquisite torture of being near him and not being able to see any tomorrows in his eyes, but the prospect of leaving him was its own kind of torture. Two more days and then what?

Back to the life she'd been content with just three short weeks ago. And now she wasn't. Because there would be no Ethan in that life.

Moreover, she couldn't even afford to dwell on her pain right now. After yesterday's mess, she really had to perfect her act.

Fear nested in her soul. Rising from her chair, she paced the study. She fought with the lists of the elite and where they had their second homes and their summer homes and their homes on foreign soil. The words blurred, and she tried again, whispering to herself as she paced.

"Adeline Darby. From Connecticut. Lives here from April through September. Winters in Palm Beach. Has homes in San Luis Obispo and Vermont. Geoffrey Lamont…"

Her mind drew a blank. She tried again. "Geoffrey Lamont, Geoffrey Lamont…" She couldn't think of a thing. Tipping back her head in anguish, Maggie closed her eyes.

"You'll be fine when the time comes. You're just pushing yourself too hard. Come."

Maggie turned around. Ethan was holding out his hand.

"Where are we going?"

"Out of here. We're escaping." One side of his mouth quirked up in a conspiratorial half smile. "You need serious escape time, bright eyes."

Where didn't really matter, anyway. Not when Ethan would be her companion. And so a scant half hour later, Maggie found herself on the lake in a sailboat. Alone with Ethan. It was the closest she was ever going to come to heaven, so she had better enjoy it while she could. Heaven would be pulling up to the shore in a few hours, and she'd be disembarking.

This had been a good idea, Ethan thought, once he'd anchored the boat well away from the shore. Sailing a boat required skill and activity, and during the time when they'd been sailing out here, there'd been no time to worry about their problems. And now that they were here…well, the boat was much too exposed for him to do something forbidden like touch her.

The ache to do just that was always there, but right now all he wanted was for Maggie to be able to relax, let down her guard and concentrate on the sun on the water and the waves lapping the boat.

"Is this better?" he asked, watching her lift her face to the sun as the golden rays heated her skin.

"This is almost better than chocolate," she said. "Or maybe it *is* better than chocolate. I could stay out here forever."

So could he. Here there was only the two of them. There were no tags. No Ethan the businessman and Maggie the custodian, no boss and employee.

"Ah, but it gets better," he said, reaching into a cooler he had brought on board just before they set sail. Digging down deep, he came up with what he was looking for—a bright red box.

Maggie tilted her head, waiting, excitement in her eyes. Like Poe, he thought with a smile.

Ethan smiled slyly. He removed the lid from the box, revealing four perfect rows of Belgian chocolates.

"A day on the lake and chocolate," he announced with a grin. "What more could a woman want?"

For two seconds they gazed at each other, and Ethan knew Maggie's thoughts mirrored his own. There was one more thing that a woman might want, and definitely something else that a man would want. This man wanted to kiss Maggie very much.

But she blinked, shaking off the moment. Eagerly she moved closer, and he took a chocolate from the box. When she parted her lips, he slipped the creamy candy inside.

The look on her face was pure ecstasy, and he caught his breath. She slowly savored the candy, then looked up at him.

"You think of everything, don't you?" she asked.

If he'd thought of everything, he would never have hired her that day at the auction. He would have known that she would prove to be the one thing he'd ever wanted that he was absolutely forbidden to have.

"I brought you something, too," she said shyly. "I thought this might be the last time I have alone with you." She reached down into her royal-blue fanny pack and pulled out a book. "I know you like roses."

The slender volume she gave him was a book on rose trivia.

He studied it carefully, the embossed leather cover, the gold lettering, and when he flipped it open, the words, "To Ethan from Maggie." Simple, uncomplicated, like Maggie herself, and so filled with meaning. Like Maggie herself.

For a few seconds he couldn't find words or breath, but finally he looked at her, the shining expectation in her eyes, the hint of worry that she had committed a faux pas. That was enough to bring his voice back in a rush.

"This is the perfect gift, Maggie," he said, his voice deepening with conviction. "And you managed to do this when? Between repairing my house, dress fittings, lessons and making sure that Poe has his daily dose of affection?"

She shrugged. "Walter helped me find it," she confessed. "I thought you'd notice if I slipped away."

Oh, she was so right, Ethan thought gazing down into eyes that suddenly held a hint of uncharacteristic shyness. He would notice if she slipped away. He had a terrible feeling that he was going to notice her absence far too much once she was gone.

"I'll treasure it," he told her. "And I'll think of you whenever I enter the garden."

She smiled then, the lake's beauty paling in comparison.

"Would you like to learn how to sail?" he asked her suddenly.

"Do you mean it? Could I do that?" The anticipation in her voice and in her eyes was so exquisitely Maggie that his breath caught in his throat. She practically wriggled with excitement. She definitely glowed.

"I believe you could do anything," he said truthfully as he took her hand and began to teach her one last lesson. Together they set about making their last moments special.

"Ethan?" Maggie asked a short time later after she'd somewhat awkwardly tried her hand at the art of tacking and had settled back to let him take them back to shore.

He simply turned to look at her, a question in his eyes.

"What if I fail you tomorrow night?"

"You'll still be Maggie. I'll still be Ethan," he said gently.

"Yes, but I wonder what that means," she said a bit sadly.

He wasn't sure he knew himself, but he knew he wasn't the same man he'd been a few weeks earlier.

"I think it means I'll miss you," he answered.

And she looked up into his eyes. Her own were clouded and unreadable, so unlike her normal self. And she didn't say anything.

It was definitely time to go back. Maggie needed to make her preparations for tomorrow.

The event they'd planned for was at hand.

Lionel's ballroom was the most beautiful, exotic room she'd ever been in, Maggie couldn't help thinking as she stood beside Ethan in the receiving line the next evening. As she was introduced to the elite of the Chicago area, she tried to pretend these were just ordinary people.

Tonight she would either save Ethan or fail him. She would also lose him. The thought brought a lump of pain to her throat that threatened to steal her voice and bring tears to her eyes. She blinked rapidly and swallowed hard.

"I'm delighted to make your acquaintance," she somehow managed to say, daintily taking the hand of the woman who'd just been introduced to her. Maggie couldn't for the life of her remember who the woman was. She hoped it didn't matter. "It's so good of you to come," she continued, speaking to the next person in line, and her comment drew a polite smile.

She was intensely aware of Ethan at her side and of the jealous looks the women gave her, but she had no time to do anything except keep mouthing platitudes. The line never seemed to end. Her feet were beginning to kill her. She didn't care. She was doing this for Ethan and, like the little mermaid, she would have given up her tongue and walked on knives for him. If the line went on for hours more, she would stand here without complaint. But then she reached out for the hand of the next person and realized that no one was there.

Turning, she finally allowed herself to look at Ethan.

"Are you all right?" he asked gently.

She nodded, wordless.

"Are you sure?"

She nodded again.

"Maggie, could you qualify that with a yes?" he whispered low so that no one could hear. "It's not like you to be silent, and if you don't say something I'm going to assume you're not all right at all. I'm going to carry you out of here in front of the mayor and everyone in the room." His look was stern, his eyes loaded with concern.

She smiled brilliantly. "I'm fine," she chirped.

His frown grew deeper. "I'm not one of those people in the audience," he told her, and he advanced slightly, fully looking as if he were going to throw her over his shoulder and carry her off like a child.

And everything he'd worked for and wanted would be ruined.

Hastily she touched his sleeve and looked up at him earnestly. "I'm just a little tired, but I'm really fine, Ethan," she whispered urgently.

"You're sure?" He looked doubtful.

"You want me to do a cartwheel?"

Silent laughter touched his eyes. "Maybe just a waltz," he said, holding out his hand to her. "Would you care to retire to the dance floor, Ms. Todd? I believe the dancing is about to begin," he said, more loudly this time.

"I love to waltz," she said eagerly. Maybe a bit too eagerly, she thought, trying to still the urge to ask Ethan if she could waltz with him all night. When Walter had taught her the dance, she'd been entranced.

She'd also been a bit overly enthusiastic, forgetting that she was supposed to let Walter lead and that it was supposed to be a graceful dance, not a wild romp. Now, though, she had even more to worry about. The thought of waltzing with Ethan nearly made her faint with longing. She'd dreamed of it.

Somehow, without quite knowing how, she was in his arms, whirling about the floor. She wanted to lean close and breathe in his scent, to enjoy every second of being this close to him, but she couldn't. Her evening had a purpose, and it wasn't to fantasize about living in Ethan's arms. If she allowed herself to do that, she'd fail him.

Tension gripped her. For two seconds she realized she was taking over, trying to lead. The thought made her falter. Unsure how to stop, she tripped on the hem of her dress.

Ethan caught her easily, gently covering up her slip and easing her back into the moves. He took control and gazed straight into her eyes.

"Maggie, sweetheart, relax. Please. It's just me," he whispered, leaning in just close enough for her to hear but far enough away that no one would wonder why he was behaving with such impropriety.

"I feel like a stick of dynamite waiting to accidentally explode," she confessed.

"Why? You've utterly charmed everyone you've met so far."

"Except for Mr. Morton," she said. "You might not have noticed, since you were talking to his daughter, but I forgot myself and stared at his hair. I'm sure that it was a toupee. I'm equally sure that he noticed me staring. Then I said something stupid like, 'I've never seen hair that exact shade of red before.' I think he's found me out."

"Not a chance. He's looking this way now. That isn't anger or indignation I see in his eyes, either, angel. The man has definitely lost his heart."

She gazed up at him. "Thank you. I know you're trying to make me feel more at ease."

"I'm trying to tell you the truth. You're magic tonight, Maggie. Every man wants to meet you. Every woman wishes she could be like you."

"That's a first," she said with a soft, self-conscious laugh.

"But it won't be the last. You're a magnificent woman, Maggie. Why don't you know that? Men should have been telling you that all your life."

She considered his question. "I don't think men have often thought of me as a woman. I was raised with men, I work with men, I do what some consider a man's job."

"If men don't see you as a woman, then they're wearing dark sunglasses. Every man here tonight knows you are very beautiful, very desirable."

"That's nice," she said shyly. "Maybe it's just that you've shown me what I can be."

"What is that?"

"More than I was."

He shook his head. "You were already more than you thought you were. Now take my arm, Maggie. I'm going to allow some other man to sample the joys of sharing your time."

He whirled her about, and her breath caught. She looked up and saw only Ethan with the world spinning around her, but she wasn't scared or disoriented. It was wildly exhilarating to twirl in his arms. She thought she could have done that forever, but the music came to an end. Ethan waltzed her to a stop right next to a small crowd of people.

"I believe you indicated that you wished for a dance with Ms. Todd?" she heard Ethan ask someone.

"I'd be a fool not to," the man said.

"Magdelena?" Ethan said, and she could tell that he was giving her an option. She could dance or she could say no.

She would never say no when she had come here to help Ethan by saying yes.

Dutifully Maggie smiled. She turned to see who her next partner would be and stepped straight into the arms of the mayor of the city.

She was an instant hit, Ethan thought. Magdalena Todd, great-great-granddaughter of the Duke of Tarrington. No one questioned her authenticity, no suspicious eyebrows were raised. And why should that be surprising? She looked every inch a woman who was of noble blood. She was a goddess, a siren, a woman who could make a man want to commit illegal acts to win her attention.

"What do you think, Lionel?" he asked, coming up behind the man. But Lionel didn't answer. He was focused on Maggie. He looked as if it would kill him to take his eyes off her.

"Lionel?"

Finally the man responded, looking back over his shoulder.

"I heard the mayor asked her to his dinner party," he said, a gleeful note in his voice. "Isn't she something, though?"

She was more than something, Ethan thought. But then, he was in love with her. The utter truth of that kicked him in the head. He was in love with Maggie Todd. Completely in love. And by the sound of

Lionel's voice, what he felt for Maggie was more than just mere admiration, too.

"She's magnificent," he agreed, but by then Lionel had gone back to his Maggie gazing. It was clear that he was pleased with the results of this evening, but for the life of him, now that they were here at the goal, Ethan couldn't connect what he was reading on Lionel's face with his plans for his restaurants. He supposed Lionel was happy to know that Ethan could deliver what he promised, but what Ethan was seeing was more than mere satisfaction.

There was pride. Affection. Longing. Lionel looked as if he'd found a lost treasure and didn't quite know how to claim it.

And Lionel was the man who had chosen Maggie at the auction.

Don't be silly, Ethan told himself. You're imagining things. Just because *you're* besotted by Maggie, you think that every other man is, too.

Just then Lionel closed his eyes. He blinked, and Ethan could swear that the man was trying to hold back tears.

"I think we should talk," Ethan told Lionel, and his mind was a whirl of sensations. What was this all about? Why *had* Lionel chosen Maggie? He'd been looking for someone who was a challenge, he'd said, but underneath the scruffy hair, the baggy dress, the chewing gum and the blue-collar upbringing, there had been a pretty framework. She'd been a challenge, but she hadn't been hopeless. There had been other women at the auction who would have been more difficult to pass off.

But Lionel had insisted on Maggie. Ethan wondered that he hadn't questioned Lionel's choice before. Maybe because he'd wanted Maggie to be the one, too.

Anger at himself and Lionel swirled through him. Something was afoot here and it wasn't right. They had played with Maggie's mind and her sense of self, and he was pretty damn sure that both of them had done it with ulterior motives.

Side by side, he marched with Lionel, into the man's library.

"You want to tell me just why Maggie was the one?" he asked, taking the direct path.

Lionel studied the question. "I might as well," he finally said, "now that we've reached the end of the road and you've done what I needed you to do."

"Which was making everyone think she was something she isn't."

"Which was making her into what she was destined to be but never had the opportunity to become," Lionel said decisively.

Alarms began to go off in Ethan's head. "You want to explain that?"

For a moment Lionel got a devilish gleam in his eyes. "Why not? I'll be explaining it to the whole world soon. Everyone's going to be quite confused to find out that Maggie isn't related to a duke at all."

Ethan frowned. "You'd do that to her?"

"And to you," Lionel admitted, "but I wouldn't worry. I have plenty of clout in this town, Ethan. I'm not only an extremely wealthy and influential man, my late wife was born into one of the leading Chicago families. Old money. Prestige. She outranked most of the people here tonight. She was a sweet woman, too. I was always glad that she died and missed the ugliness that my daughter and I went through."

Ethan wasn't completely following, though a strong sense of dread was overtaking him. He shook his head.

"I take it that you're going to drop a bombshell here. Am I right, Lionel?"

The grumpy old man smiled. He opened a desk drawer and pulled out a photo of a young woman. She looked like him in many ways, except for the fullness of her lips and the eagerness in her eyes.

Ethan reached for a chair and slumped into it. "Your daughter," he said, not needing to ask, and he didn't need to ask how Maggie tied into this, either. Most people might not notice, but most people hadn't spent hours gazing at her the way he had. Maggie was clearly related to the woman in the picture.

"You have a lot of explaining to do, Lionel," he said hoarsely, "and what you have to say had better not hurt Maggie."

"How could it? She's about to find out that she's a rich young woman, the actual granddaughter of one of Chicago's leading families. No pretense this time."

"And how did she end up where she is if you're such a loving grandfather?" Ethan barked out the question.

Lionel's smile disappeared. He slumped into a chair opposite Ethan. "Her mother...well, her grandmother had died. I was raising Darlene alone. She was angry at things that had happened between her mother and me before my wife's death, she was rebellious and began seeing a series of men who weren't...well, they had no connections. We argued. She thought she was in love. She ended up pregnant. I...I threw her out of the house. No one else knew about the baby."

"No one wondered what happened to your daughter?"

Lionel raised tortured eyes. "I thought you knew me better than that."

"You keep a low personal profile."

The old man nodded slowly. "You mean I tell people to get the hell out of my business. Yes, well, I told people that Darlene had moved overseas. Years later I tried to find her, but she had covered her tracks well, I thought. Actually, she'd died. The baby had vanished into the system. It didn't matter. With Darlene gone, I didn't want anything to do with the child. But you get old, you realize you have no family. Or maybe you *do* have a family if you could only change the past. It took me years of lying and cheating to find out where she was."

"And you found her not far from home, but you didn't tell her the truth."

"I had thrown her mother out of the house. Darlene had died in childbirth. If she'd had the kind of care I could have paid for, she'd be alive. And besides, you saw what Maggie was. Do you think she would have welcomed the connection?"

Hot anger raced through Ethan. "What she was, was an extraordinary woman."

"Because she's a Griggs."

The man's arrogance was beyond belief. "Because she's Maggie, and she was raised with love and caring."

"She was raised poor and with no sense of society. You've changed that now. Now I can smooth things over with everyone. They'll forgive her for the deception. She can come home now."

Ethan didn't trust himself to speak. He couldn't rise for fear he would become a violent man and harm someone who was too old and physically weak to defend himself, so he clenched the arms of the chair.

He wanted to tell Lionel to leave Maggie alone, but he had no right. She was an adult, Lionel *was* her grandfather, like it or not. He didn't even have the right to tell her the truth, and he wasn't sure he could deliver the message, anyway. Would she welcome it?

Or would she be hurt? So much of her past kept from her. The ugliness of what had happened between Lionel and her mother. The knowledge that Lionel had known who she was and hadn't wanted to claim her without first changing her.

Ethan gritted his teeth. "I'm taking Maggie home tonight," he told Lionel, pushing out of his chair.

"You'll tell her."

"That's not my right. If you want to destroy her illusions, you'll have to do it without me."

Lionel chortled. "Destroy her illusions? She'll be a woman of privilege from now on. Men will seek her out."

The blow nearly sent Ethan spinning back into his chair. Maggie would be a marital prize, dollar signs and prestige all tied up in a beautiful package. And he'd helped do that to her. He'd practiced what had seemed like a harmless deception and had ended up manipulating Maggie for Lionel's purposes.

And maybe in the end she would welcome the results. She would, after all, have what many women would envy.

Men would desire her and pursue her.

And she would think it was only because of her newfound position and money. Not a single man could expect her to think anything else. Not even him.

Ethan closed his eyes and felt the pain building. He realized he had hoped that once all was done, once Maggie was back in her world, he might renew their acquaintance without pretense or plan this time, that they might begin afresh.

That couldn't happen now.

He turned on his heel and left the room without another word. He only hoped he could keep Maggie from noticing the furious cyclone of emotion and regret building inside of him.

Chapter Twelve

Something was wrong. That was all Maggie could think when she saw Ethan making his way across the room. His eyes were fierce, his expression was thunderous. And when he saw her, she could see the effort it took for him to calm himself.

"You've done a beautiful job tonight, Magdalena," he said, his voice softer than usual. "I hope you've gotten at least some enjoyment out of all this." Still he didn't smile.

That bothered her. This should be his moment of triumph. "What's not to enjoy?" she asked teasingly. "I danced with the mayor. A lot of other men, too. Most of them were just silly, but it was pretty entertaining."

"You should get to dance more often."

She shrugged and grinned. "I dance all the time. With my broom and mop. They're actually not bad partners, either. They let me lead," she whispered conspiratorially.

But still he didn't smile. "Are you tired? All those hours on your feet."

She gingerly lifted the skirt of her gown, letting her low green pumps show through. "I've been practicing with the heels in my room," she confessed in a whisper. "So I was okay with these low ones. Still, I *am* just a bit tired."

"I'll get you home," he said gently, sliding his hand beneath her arm. "You're probably anxious to go."

She wasn't. The thought that she was on the verge of leaving him, pressed down on her painfully. She tried to shut out the suffocating fear that she would never see him again, but she couldn't. And Ethan seemed eager to be rid of her now that the ball was almost over.

"I'm packed," she said quietly. "Just let me go back to Bennington Manor and change out of this dress."

His jaw seemed to grow tighter. "Of course." And he led her from the Griggs mansion.

The ride home was silent, an oddity between them. It wasn't a comfortable silence, either. Soon Maggie was back at his home, changed, and he was carrying her things to his car. In less time than she believed possible, she was in front of her tiny apartment, and her life was about to return to normal.

As if that would ever be possible—because now she knew Ethan existed, and he would always be out of reach.

Silently he helped her from the car and saw her to her door as agony began to build inside her. Somehow she fumbled for her key, unlocked the door and turned to him after he'd slipped her bag inside the door. She felt as if her very life was walking away from her, she could barely breathe for the pain, but he mustn't see that. If he thought she was another Vanessa, a woman dying for him to love her, it would shatter him.

"I...I guess this is it, then. The end of the show," she said, trying for brightness.

He gazed down at her. For a moment she thought he was going to speak, but he silently reached out and slid his hands around her waist. He pulled her to him and placed his lips over hers. Softly, so very softly—though she could feel his hunger.

The pain was exquisite, the need to hold on to him intense. She fought back her tears and willed her body to stay still.

Finally he drew back.

"Be happy, bright eyes. Have a wonderful life."

And then she was inside and Ethan was gone. She was glad. If he'd stayed, she might have broke down and told him that the most wonderful part of her life had just driven away.

Well, it was done, Ethan had thought that night when he'd come home, and he was still thinking the same thing three days later. But he couldn't get Maggie out of his mind. She'd made him believe in the possibility of things he'd always scorned. Love and hope and simple pleasures and lasting, happy families.

"*Rubbish,*" he said out loud. It didn't matter. There was no one there to hear but Poe, and he was inconsolable, too. When they went out for their evening romp, there was less vigor in the big dog's step. And Walter? He was beginning to look stooped and old instead of quietly efficient.

"I've heard she's got suitors lining her driveway," Ethan told the big dog who had come up to him, waiting for him to scratch his ears. Ethan slid down the wall and sat next to the animal, doing as his pet wished. Poe let out a soft rumble.

"I know. It's not the same when Maggie isn't here to see to you, is it, boy?" he asked. "There's no life in the house."

But things had worked out for Maggie. The mayor had decided that her charade was entertaining. Even Sylvia had pretended to be amused, although he was reasonably sure that she just didn't want to be the only one left out of the joke. In the end, everyone had decided that the mysterious gift of Lionel's granddaughter coming into their midst was more exciting than it would have been had Maggie actually been related to a duke they'd never heard of. And now Maggie might soon be falling in love with one of the men who was courting her.

Ethan clenched his fingers, and Poe barked.

"I'm sorry," Ethan said, soothing the fur he'd accidentally tugged at. "Look at me, I'm a lost man, Poe. I've told Maggie over and over that I don't want love, so why should she believe that it's different with her? Why would she think that I want her for herself and not because she's suddenly changed her colors and elevated her social status?"

When Walter came in, Ethan and the big dog were both looking at each other mournfully. Neither of them had come up with any grand ideas to bring Maggie back home.

If one more man told her that her eyes reminded him of brown velvet or asked her where she had been hiding all his life, Maggie thought she just might kick him in the shins. Wouldn't Lionel like that?

She almost smiled. Lionel had gone to such pains to make sure she learned how to be respectable and yet he really hadn't been able to change much about her, definitely not her thoughts. She wondered what he'd say if she told him that she unhooked her phone now and then, just to give herself a rest from all those men he seemed so pleased about.

When he'd shown up at her door the morning after the ball and told her about her parents, she probably should have been shocked or angry or even excited. No doubt once the truth really sank in, she would be some of those things and more. But she'd lived so long without a past, she'd made her peace with the mystery of her birth. Her father and brothers *were* her real family. Besides, Ethan had so filled her heart and mind that she couldn't concentrate on anything else. All she could feel was a mild sense of surprise, a bit of disorientation and some genuine sadness for Lionel, who'd obviously still not learned what mattered most in life.

The only thing that had gotten through to her was Lionel's anger this morning because Ethan was refusing to work with him. He'd turned down the offer that had been the reason for this whole arrangement.

Because of *her,* Lionel had said. And that bothered her. A lot. Ethan needed Lionel's business.

She wondered what Ethan would say if she called him up and asked him to take Lionel's account.

"I can't," she said between frozen lips. If she called him, her throat would close up and she wouldn't be able to speak. Or worse, she'd end up crying. And she never cried. Ethan would think she was dying.

"Well, aren't you?" she whispered. But still she couldn't pick up the phone or even reconnect it.

In her mind she heard her father chastising her, "Maggie, girl, be strong," in his no-nonsense voice that had sounded a bit weaker when he'd discovered that she had a rich well-known grandfather. She'd hugged him and told him that he was the most important man in her life, but even that upset him.

"You won't stop coming to visit us now that you're important?" he asked.

"Try and keep me away. I'll beat down your door," she promised.

But it was Ethan's door she longed for right now. And Ethan's well-being. It was cowardly not to call when she was so worried about him.

She went to the phone.

What if there was a woman with Ethan?

Pain squeezed at her heart, but this wasn't about her. It was about him. He'd earned his reward and darn it, she wanted him to have it. Hadn't he given her lectures on taking care of herself the whole time she was at his house? It was time she gave a few orders. He was not going to make some silly sacrifice because he felt that Lionel had wronged her.

Self-righteous anger gave her courage, and Maggie hurriedly plugged in the phone and lifted the receiver before she could change her mind.

Walter picked up the phone on the second ring. Dear, sweet Walter. His voice triggered a waterfall of emotions she tried to hold back.

"Wal-ter?" Maggie asked in a quivery voice. And then she lost it completely. "I'm…I'm here," she was trying to say when he questioned her, but she couldn't stop the rush of tears. "Is Ethan there?" she managed to say.

"I'm afraid not," he said gently.

"I…I—" She knew she'd never get the courage to do this again.

"He tried to call you yesterday and last night and this morning. He's on his way to your house. Let me patch you through to his cell phone, my dear."

Oh, yes. Oh no, she thought. If he saw the mess her house was in, he'd know just how miserable she'd been these past few days. Then he'd never make peace with Lionel.

"Goodbye, Walter," she said, hanging up the phone. She looked around madly at her apartment. Ethan was on the way. He was coming to see her because she'd stupidly disconnected the phone. Her house was a mess, but her heart was even more of a mess and she had to do something so he wouldn't know she was so crazy in love with him that she was insane and—

The doorbell rang.

Maggie raced to the door. She threw it open. She launched herself forward straight at Ethan. No. The man staring back at her wasn't Ethan. He was another of those cookie-cutter rich men.

The flowers he was carrying smashed against her chest and he roped his skinny arms around her.

"No." She looked at him in shock and pushed back, but he smiled and held on as she braced her hands against his chest, keeping him as far away as possible.

Somewhere in the background a car door slammed. Maggie looked up, straight into Ethan's silver eyes. He was tall, his black hair was more gorgeous than she remembered, his scowl was black as sin, but he was here. A tear slid down her cheek.

The young man turned around, and Ethan gave him a look that might have turned him to ashes if he'd stood there for two seconds.

"I'm...sorry," he stammered. "I didn't know she was yours." And he backed away, then ran to his car.

Ethan looked down at Maggie. "You didn't answer your phone. I thought something was wrong. I was afraid you were hurt." And there was such accusation and sorrow in his voice, such pain in her own heart that Maggie closed her eyes as the tears trickled down.

"Maggie? Oh, Maggie, don't cry. I'm sorry I chased your young man away."

The tears fell more freely.

"Maggie?"

"I am—" The words *so in love with you* stuck in her throat. "I am so mad at you," she finally said. "You turned down my grandfather's business."

"I know."

"That was wrong."

"He hurt you. There's no reason he couldn't have told you the truth from the start."

"I can handle Lionel's insensitivity. I've dealt with plenty of thoughtless men in my lifetime, but you...you *need* that business."

"Not that much."

"I don't want you making this sacrifice for me," she pleaded.

"You're not even angry with him?" he asked.

She twisted her fingers together. "I am, but most of my anger is tied up with things he did before I was born, and maybe when I was first born, and that was long ago. And even if he did awful things, he suffered for them, and he's still suffering. I haven't welcomed him yet."

"Because he hurt you." Ethan's voice was like a knife slash.

She dared to place her fingers on his arm and felt the warmth of skin beneath white cotton. The shock of touching him again was so wonderful that she could barely find her voice. "Not because I'm hurt," she managed to say. "Because I need to think of my family, too. This is a delicate situation."

Ethan brushed his knuckles across her cheek. "I

don't know how anyone could ever have believed that you weren't a lady. You have more sensitivity in you than any woman I've ever met. Do you want me to go chase down your young man?''

She bit her lip and shook her head, sure that he was going to leave now.

''I—'' He looked to the side. ''Lionel tells me that you have lots of male traffic lately. Do they all bring you flowers?''

''Some.'' She didn't want to talk about those men. Not when Ethan was here.

He frowned. ''Yesterday, last night, this morning when you didn't answer your phone, I— Damn it, Maggie, I was afraid you were hurt. Was it…one of those men? Was that the reason I couldn't get through?''

He looked like he wanted to pound a wall. ''I'm sorry,'' he said. ''That isn't my business. If you've met someone you want to marry, that's your private affair.''

She almost gasped, it hurt so much to know he didn't care. But she shook her head vehemently. ''I'm not getting married.''

''You told me that before,'' he whispered. ''I should have remembered. And believed. Be happy, Maggie.'' And he kissed her on the cheek. She closed her eyes, and one lone tear trickled down her cheek.

''Maggie?''

She couldn't look at him. ''I'm sorry. I never cry. It's just—well, I got used to you and…you and Walter and Poe. I guess I've missed you. I don't do change real well.''

''I don't do change real well, either,'' he admitted.

She looked up into his eyes. Another tear escaped.

''Maggie, don't.'' And Ethan bent and kissed her tears. He lifted her into his arms and sat down on the stairs with her.

"I'm sorry. If you're mad at me about Lionel, I'll patch it up with him. I'll do whatever you want, only don't cry, sweetheart. You're killing me."

She hid her face against his chest. It felt so good to be surrounded by him. And she couldn't stop the tears.

"It's not Lionel," she gasped.

"Is it the missing Walter and Poe...and me?"

She tried to nod against his chest. He held her close.

"Come with me." And he rose, taking her with him.

"Where?"

He hesitated.

She waited. For a moment he looked away, but then he turned back to her. "Maybe we ended things too suddenly. I know this beautiful garden. It's a nice place to find strength and peace. And you can see Walter and Poe, too."

Oh, yes. Longing filled her, but she shouldn't do this. Going back where she'd fallen in love with him and then leaving again would only double the pain.

But she gazed up into his eyes and said yes.

He smiled, and her world righted itself for a while. A short time later she was back in the rose garden. She fell to her knees and drank in the sweet scent of roses.

Ethan dropped to his knees beside her. He picked a yellow rose and removed the thorns. Carefully he slipped it into her hair.

"I've been wanting to do that for a long time," he admitted. "I suppose I'm no better than the guy I chased away today."

He was so much better than any man.

"Why did you try to call me?" she asked suddenly. "What did you want?"

He sadly shook his head. "What every man seems to want. Come see."

And he drew her to her feet and led her to the white-

and-green gazebo covered with trailing red roses. In the center of the gazebo was a silver trunk. Ethan opened it and tipped back the lid.

When he stepped aside she almost thought that he was nervous. She peered in and found a lush hodge-podge of high heels. Silver. Gold. Green. Red. Lilac. All colors. All delicate, and only one shoe of each pair.

She shook her head, confused. She didn't know what was going on here. It was something new. Ethan had shown her so many new things. Wonderful things.

"I don't understand," she said.

"Don't try to." And he knelt at her feet. He slipped her shoe off, his palm brushing against her skin, and she caught her breath and held it.

He looked up into her eyes, then reached into the trunk, pulling out a lacy red heel. He gazed into her eyes as he began to place it on her foot.

"What are you doing?" Her voice was a mere shadow of her normal speech.

"Courting you," he said softly. "You have men courting you, don't you?"

She almost didn't dare to breathe. She couldn't answer.

Ethan took her hand and kissed the inside of her wrist, and her pulse began to flutter. "I'm no better than that guy on your porch. I'm no different, Maggie. When I tried to call you, I had some crazy thought of trying to find some way of convincing you that we needed to spend more time together. Poe and I have spent a lot of time roaming shoe stores these past few days, trying to forget you, collecting all of these. I have all the mates." He indicated the trunk of shoes. "If I gave you a pair a day, it would take a while before we reached the bottom, and if I ran out, I'd get more."

"You wanted to spend more time with me, and you were going to bribe me with shoes?"

He smiled sheepishly. "You like high heels," he reminded her.

"Yes, they're my weakness. One of my weaknesses, anyway."

Ethan's eyes turned dark. "What are your other weaknesses?"

He leaned close. She knew she should move away. She was about to do something incredibly stupid. "You're my weakness. My worst weakness," she admitted. "And why not? I'm just like every other woman in the world."

"No. You're not like any other woman at all."

How could he not know? "Don't you know what effect you have on women?"

"I don't care what effect I have on women. Only on you."

Her breath caught in her throat. For a minute all she could do was look at him as a tear slipped from beneath her lashes. Ethan swore and gently wiped the tear away with his thumb. Only this time it was a tear of joy.

"You're not like other men, either." She choked out the words. "What other man would turn my grandfather's business down when you need it?"

"It's not that important to me anymore. Someone taught me there were other things that mattered more than business. Come back to me, Maggie? Be my lady again?"

He wanted her to play the game longer. She didn't think she could be that close and not fall apart with loving him. "No, I can't. I never was much of a lady. I never really wanted to be a lady."

Ethan closed his eyes. "I'm sorry. I never meant to hurt you or put pressure on you, Maggie."

"You're not…hurting me," she managed to choke out. "It's just—couldn't I just be yours for a little while longer?"

A low groan escaped Ethan. He pulled her close, sliding his hands into her hair as they both knelt on the carpeting of the gazebo. Slowly he brought his lips to hers and kissed her just once. He shook his head. "That wouldn't work for me."

Her heart broke in ten thousand pieces.

Ethan brushed his lips against her ear. "I'm greedy, Maggie. I want you for always. I don't ever want to let you go again," he whispered against her skin. "I love you so much it's an ache within me. I don't know how I've made it though these past few days without you."

"It was awful."

"It was absolute hell. And I know—well, you've told me often enough—that you don't need a man, but do you think you could ever consider marrying me?"

She couldn't answer right away. She wondered if he was asking her out of some sense of misplaced guilt, but the emotion in those dark silver eyes told her all she needed to know.

She laid her cheek against his chest. "I love you, Ethan. I couldn't marry anyone else. That's why I took my phone off the hook, because I didn't want to talk to all those other men. I guess I was just waiting for you. So you don't have to bribe me. You're all I want. You can even take the shoes back," she offered. "You're sure this is what you want?"

And she leaned back to look in his eyes. He was smiling and shaking his head. "Now I know you love me. Take back the shoes? No other woman could do them justice. No other woman could ever replace you,

Maggie, my heart, my love." Slowly he rose, drawing her to her feet.

Then he set her away from him. He reached into his pocket and produced the mate to the red heel. Carefully he slipped it on her other foot. Then, taking her hands in his own, he gave a gentle tug, tumbling her into his arms. His lips claimed hers in a slow, commanding kiss.

When he raised his head, she was flushed and smiling. "Ethan?" She looked into his eyes.

He waited.

"Does this mean you'll make love to me soon?"

He groaned and pulled her close. "As soon as possible."

"Good," she said, kissing his chin, his eyes, his lips. "Because much as I love the shoes, I love being in your arms more. When you kiss me, you make my head spin."

Ethan raised one brow. "I make your head spin, do I?"

"You always did."

He grinned and brushed his knuckles against her cheek. "If I'd only known."

"You know now," she whispered. "What…what do *I* do for you?"

He framed her face with his hands. "You complete me."

And then his mouth covered hers and the world began to spin away.

Epilogue

The arguing in the rose garden was rising to a fevered pitch. Ethan watched and listened in amazement as Maggie's father and her grandfather each tried to make his point.

"I say the baby should be named Nathaniel. It's an old family name," Lionel insisted.

"Well, Maggie is just as much my family as she ever was yours, and I think she should name the baby Jonathan. It's a good, strong name." Matthew Todd looked as if he was going to start pounding on something to get his way. Lionel was turning an unattractive shade of pink.

"Let's just leave them to enjoy themselves," Maggie whispered, and Ethan couldn't help chuckling.

"Do you think we should tell them that we're having twins?" he wondered. "Plenty of babies to love and plenty to name."

"Are you kidding?" Maggie said, shaking her head and kissing her husband on the cheek before she tiptoed

out of the garden after him. "And spoil their fun? They
love arguing."

He grinned and agreed as he slipped his arm around
her waist. "Good, then we'll leave them to it, love."
He pulled her body tight against his and kissed her
hard, angling his lips over hers.

"Um, do you know what I like doing, Mr. Bennington?" she asked, fluttering her eyelashes up at him.

He kissed her neck, and she leaned back in his arms,
letting her head fall back to accommodate him. "Oh,
I do," he agreed. "You love fixing the plumbing."

She chuckled and swatted at him, then raised her
head and gave him the look, that high-born-lady look
that Walter had taught her.

Ethan grinned. "Oh, you mean the thing *I* love the
most, too."

"Making miracles happen?" she teased, sliding her
leg up against his.

Ethan stilled his movements and wondered what his
wife was up to.

"You *did* make a miracle happen with me, Ethan,"
she said.

"You *are* a miracle, my love, my lady, my wife.
And the thing I love the most in life is making love
with you."

"Ah, but I'm not really a lady," she confessed.

"You're everything. You're my lady, you're my
friend, you're the woman who fixes my plumbing, who
steals my heart, who makes my pulse pound faster
when you do that eyelash flutter that Walter taught you
and who rules my nights. I need you, Maggie. I love
you beyond belief, everything that you are, ever have
been and ever will be."

Her arms came up about his neck. She touched her
lips to his. "Then tonight I'd like to be your seductress.

I know where there's an empty room with a bed. It would be a shame to waste that. Meet me upstairs in ten minutes?''

"Why ten minutes?''

She kissed his chin and smiled against his skin. "I think maybe my father and grandfather *are* getting a bit louder. Maybe you'd better go tell them the good news about the twins. I want my children to grow up with both a grandfather and a great-grandfather. That won't happen if they kill each other now.''

Ethan laughed as he took her lips one more time. "Ten minutes. No more,'' he agreed.

But when he arrived in their bedroom ten minutes later, the room was empty.

He smiled and pulled out what he'd gathered after making short work of Lionel and Matthew. Carefully he sprinkled rose petals on the sheets. He lit white candles in crystal holders because he knew that Maggie loved the illusion of nighttime during the afternoon.

"I'll be right there, Ethan.'' Maggie's soft voice came from the other room. It made him ache to hold her as it always did. So Ethan lay back and waited for the woman of his heart to appear. If it were necessary, he realized, he would have waited forever for her. She was the only woman who had ever been able to do that to him.

And as she entered the room, wearing a lacy white negligee and a man-killer pair of nearly bare high heels, his breath caught in his throat. Some things just got better with love.

When she saw the bed, she breathed in deeply.

"My favorite roses,'' she said.

"My favorite wife,'' he whispered, reaching for her. "I love you, Maggie,'' he said as she came to him and brought heaven with her.

Later they lay side by side, and he played with one silky curl that had fallen across her face.

"The brochure at the auction said you could fix anything. Who knew that it was my heart you would mend? You've brought me such joy, Maggie."

"You've taught me such magic, Ethan. And you've brought such wonderful things into my life."

"High heels?" he asked, grinning as he picked up one lacy shoe that had ended up on the bed.

"Mmm," she agreed. "And you've brought a college education for Will, you've brought me Walter and Poe, and roses and babies and love. So much love I can't wait to face each new day. I love you Ethan."

He raised one brow. "Well, since you're feeling so kindly toward me, come here, my lovely custodian."

She raised up on one elbow and grinned. "Do you need something repaired?"

He kissed her and she shivered. "All I need is you, my wife, in my arms."

"I can't think of any place I'd rather be."

Then he kissed her and tumbled his lady back into the roses.

*　*　*　*　*

And don't miss

THE BILLIONAIRE'S BARGAIN

by Myrna Mackenzie
Ethan's friend, Dylan Valentine,
needs someone to help him look after
two adorable toddlers. But when he
bids on the lovely April Pruitt, this
billionaire may get more than he
bargained for!
Coming only to
Silhouette Romance
in October 2002
For a sneak preview of this
touching story just turn the page.

Chapter One

What *was* that woman doing behind that tree? Dylan Valentine craned his neck and caught a glimpse of curly blond hair and a slender form as the lady in question peeped out from behind the trunk of an old oak. Unfortunately, the woman looked up at that moment and caught him staring at her. Blushing prettily, she popped back behind her tree.

Intriguing, Dylan thought, although it didn't really matter. She wasn't the type that he'd come here for. "Much too fragile for what I have in mind," he mumbled to himself. "I need an older woman. Preferably one made of steel."

As he crossed the green, he looked out of the corner of his eye and saw the fragile blond woman peer out from her tree again. She smiled at a group of women passing by, vacated her hiding place and slipped into their midst as they moved across the park toward the stage.

Surrounded by a large group of chattering women, the lady was just as invisible as she was behind the tree.

"What an odd woman," he muttered. On an impulse, he flipped through his brochure. April Pruitt. A high school teacher. No experience with little boys. Not what he was looking for at all.

And anyway, he really didn't have time to wonder about the woman or her strange behavior. The kindergarten teacher might be auctioned off at any time. That was the woman he was looking for. Agnes something. Very stern and capable-looking, solid. No doubt she'd know what to do with his half brothers when they arrived. He certainly didn't have a clue. He was in desperate need of Agnes and her ability to handle beings under three feet tall. She was the woman here who seemed promising.

Well, promising in the right way, Dylan thought, his gaze wandering to the group of women who'd been concealing his sprite. She had just stepped from the shelter of their midst.

Very attractive, he thought. *In an ethereal way.* Slight and slim, her dusty blond hair fell in curling layers to kiss her cheeks and swished against her shoulders. A pale yellow floral dress hinted at gentle curves beneath. It wafted around her pretty legs encased in cream-colored stockings and shoes. She had a pair of little gold glasses hanging on a golden cord around her neck and she looked pale and translucently lovely. Like a woman from a time long past.

She also looked just the tiniest bit like a woman trying to be braver than she really was.

As he watched her, she took a visibly deep breath, purposefully pushed her shoulders back, threaded her way through the crowd and stepped up on the risers at center stage.

The lady on the risers *did* interest him, Dylan admitted. But the reasons she snagged his attention were all wrong. The buttons she was pushing were personal. And best forgotten.

He wanted to turn away. He even *started* to turn away. Then he looked at her again. He took a step closer to the stage.

* * * * *

SILHOUETTE *Romance*™

Lost siblings, secret worlds,
tender seduction—live the fantasy in...

A TALE OF THE SEA

**Separated and hidden since childhood,
Phoebe, Kai, Saegar and Thalassa
must reunite in order to safeguard
their underwater kingdom.
But who will protect *them*...?**

*Look for these titles wherever
Silhouette books are sold!*

Silhouette®

Where love comes alive™

**Where royalty and romance
go hand in hand...**

The series continues in Silhouette Romance
with these unforgettable novels:

HER ROYAL HUSBAND
by Cara Colter
on sale July 2002 (SR #1600)

THE PRINCESS HAS AMNESIA!
by Patricia Thayer
on sale August 2002 (SR #1606)

SEARCHING FOR HER PRINCE
by Karen Rose Smith
on sale September 2002 (SR #1612)

And look for more Crown and Glory stories in
SILHOUETTE DESIRE starting in October 2002!

Available at your favorite retail outlet.

COMING NEXT MONTH